I0834568

STORIES AND SKETCHES.

Stories and Sketches

BY

OUR BEST AUTHORS.

BOSTON:
LEE AND SHEPARD.
1867.

CONTENTS.

The Skeleton at the Banquet.

DR. GRAHAM sat in his office, his book closed on his knee, and his eyes fixed upon the street. There was nothing of interest to be seen. A light snow was falling, making the pavement dreary; but it was Christmas, and his thoughts had gone back to other days, as people's thoughts will go on anniversary occasions. He was thinking of the young wife he had buried three years and three months ago; of the great fireplace in his boyhood's home, and his mother's face lit up by the glow; of many things past which were pleasant; and reflecting sadly upon the fact that life grew duller, more commonplace, as one grew older. Not that he was an elderly man,—he was, in reality, but twenty-eight; yet, upon that Christmas day, he felt old, very old; his wife dead, his practice slender, his prospects far from promising,—even the slow-moving days daily grew heavier, soberer, more serious. It was a holiday, but he had not even an invitation for dinner, where the happiness of friends and the free flow of thought might lend a momentary sparkle to his own stale spirits.

The doctor was not of a melancholy, despondent nature, nor did he rely for his pleasures upon others. He was a self-made man, and self-reliant to an unusual degree, as self-made men are apt to be. His tussle with circumstances had awakened in him a combative and resistant energy, which had served him well when means were scant and the rewards of merit few. But there is something in the festal character of Christmas which, by luring from the shadows of our struggle-life the boy nature of us, makes homeless men feel solitary; and, from being forlorn, the mood soon grows to one of painful unrest; all from beholding happiness from which we are shut out. On this gray afternoon not the most fascinating speculations of De Boismont and the hospital lectures, — not the consciousness of the originality and importance of his own discoveries in the field of Sensation and Nerve Force, — had any interest for Dr. Graham.

That he had talent and a good address; that he studied and experimented many hours every day; that he as thoroughly understood his profession as was consistent with a six years' actual experience as an actual practitioner; that there was nothing of the quack or pretender in him;—all this did not prevent his rent from being high, his patients few, and his means limited. With no influential friends to recommend and introduce him, he had resolutely rented a room in a genteel locality up town, had dressed well, and had worn the "air" of a man of business, ever ready for duty; but success had not attended upon his efforts, and the future gave no promise of a change. Of this he was thinking, somewhat bitterly; for what proud soul is not stung with unmerited neglect? Then a deep sadness stole over him at thoughts of the loss which had come upon his early manhood, — a loss like which there is none other so abiding in strong, wise hearts. A cloud seemed to be sifting down and closing around him, which, with unusual passivity, he seemed unable or unwilling to shake off. A carriage obstructed his view, by passing in front of his window. It stopped; then the footman descended, opened the carriage-door, and turned to the office-bell. He was followed by his master, who awaited the answer to the bell, and was ushered into the practitioner's presence by the single waiting-servant of his modest establishment. The doctor arose to receive his guest, who was a man still younger than himself, with something of a foreign air, and dressed with a quiet richness in keeping with his evident wealth and position.

"Dr. Graham?"

The doctor bowed assent.

"If you are not otherwise engaged, I would like you to go home with me, to see my sister, who is not well. There is no great haste about the matter, but if you can go now, I shall be glad to take you with me. It will save you a walk through the snow."

"He knows," thought the doctor, "that I do not drive a carriage;" and that a stranger, of such ability to hire the most noted practitioners, should call upon him, was a source of unexpressed surprise and suspicion.

"What do you think is the matter with your sister?" he unconcernedly asked, taking his overcoat from the wardrobe.

"That is for you to decide. It is a case of no ordinary character — one which will require study." He led the way at once to the door, as if unwilling to delay, notwithstanding he had at first stated that no haste was necessary. "Step in, doctor, and I will give you an inkling of the case during the drive, which will occupy some fifteen or twenty minutes."

"In the first place," continued the stranger, as they rolled away, "I will introduce myself to you as St. Victor Marchand, at present a resident of your city, but recently from the island of Madeira. My house is upon the Fifth Avenue, not far from Madison Square. My household consists only of myself and sister, with our servants. I have the means to remunerate you amply for any demands we may make upon your time or skill; and I ought to add, one reason for selecting so young a physician is, that I think you will be the more able and willing to devote more time to the case than more famous practitioners. However, you are not unknown to me. I have heard you well-spoken of; and I remember that, when you were a student in Paris, you were mentioned with honor by the college, for an able paper read before the open section upon the very subject to which I now propose to direct your attention,— mental disease," he added, after a moment's hesitation.

"A case of insanity?" bluntly asked the doctor.

"Heaven forbid! And yet I must not conceal from you that I fear it."

"Give me some of the symptoms. Insanity in strong development, or aberration of faculties, or hallucination?"

"I cannot reply. It is one and all, it seems to me. The fact is, doctor, I wish to introduce you to your patient simply as a friend of mine, so as to give you an opportunity for studying my sister's case, unembarrassed by any suspicion on her part. To excite her suspicions is to frustrate all hopes of doing anything for or with her. Can you — will you — do me the favor to dine with me this evening? It is now only about an hour to six, and if you have no other engagement, I will do my best to entertain you, and you can then meet my sister as her brother's guest. Shall it be so?"

The young man's tones were almost beseeching, and his manner betrayed the most intense solicitude. Quite ready to accede to the request, from curiosity as well as from a desire to reassure the young man, Dr. Graham did not hesitate to say, "Willingly, sir, if it will assist in a professional knowledge of the object of my call."

The change from the office to the home into which the physician was introduced was indeed grateful to the doctor's feelings. The light, warmth, and splendor of the rooms gave to the home an air of tropical sensuousness; and yet an exquisite taste seemed to preside over all. Though not unfamiliar with elegance, this home of the brother and sister wore, to the visitor, an enchanted look, as well from the foreign character of many of its adornments and the rare richness of its works of art, as from the gay, friendly, enthusiastic manner of his entertainer, — a manner never attained by English or Americans. Sending word to Miss Marchand that there would be a guest to dinner, St. Victor fell into a sparkling conversation, discoursing most intelligibly of Paris, Madeira, the East Indies, and South America, taking his guest from room to room to show this or that curious specimen of the productions or handicraft of each country. As the articles exhibited were rare, and many of them of scientific value, and as the young man's knowledge kept pace with his eloquence of discourse, Dr. Graham was agreeably absorbed.

An hour passed rapidly. Then the steward announced dinner; but it was not until they were about seating themselves at table that *the patient* made her appearance. It was now twilight out of doors. The curtains were drawn and the dining-room lit only by wax tapers, under whose soft radiance bloomed an abundance of flowers, mostly of exotic beauty and fragrance. It was evident that the young master of the house brought with him his early tastes.

"We have an extra allowance of light and flowers, and a little feast, too, I believe; for neither myself nor my English steward here forget that this is Christmas.

Don't you think it a beautiful holiday? My mother always kept it with plenty of wax candles and flowers."

"It is a sacred day to me," answered the doctor, sadly, thinking of his lost wife and of the three times they had kept it together, with feasting and love's delights.

At this moment Miss Marchand floated into the room and to her place at the head of the table,—a girlish creature, who gave their guest a smile when the brother said,—

"Dr. Graham is not entirely a stranger, Edith; he was in Paris when we were there. You were a child, then. I was indeed glad to meet him in this strange city, and I mean that we shall be friends upon a visiting footing, if he will permit it."

It was but natural for the physician to fix a piercing look upon the face of her whom he had been given to understand was to be his patient, and whose disease was of a character to command his best skill. His physician's eye detected no outward tokens of ill health, either of body or of mind. A serene brow, sweet, steady, loving eyes, cheeks rosy and full with maiden health, a slender though not thin figure, all were there before him, giving no indication even of the "nervousness" assumed to be so common with young ladies of this generation. Exquisite beauty, allied with perfect health, seemed to "blush and bloom" all over her; and the medical man would have chosen her, with professional enthusiasm, as his ideal of what a young woman *ought* to be. Her pink-silk robe adapted itself to her soft form as naturally as the petals of a rose to its curving sweetness. Only to look upon her gladdened the sad heart of Dr. Graham, the wifeless and childless. He felt younger than he had felt for years, as thirsty grass feels under the influence of a June sun after a morning of showers. His spirits rose, and he talked well, even wittily, — betraying not only his varied learning as a student and his keen powers of observation as a man of the world, but also the gentleness and grace which, in his more active, worldly life, were too much put aside. It was a little festival, in which the dainty dishes, the fruit, and wine played but a subordinate part.

Nothing could be more apparent than the pride and affection with which Mr. Marchand regarded his sister. Was there, indeed, a skeleton at this feast? The doctor shuddered as he asked himself the question. All his faculties were on the alert to deny and disprove the possibility of the presence of the hideous visitor. His sympathies were too keenly enlisted to be willing to acknowledge its existence even in the background of that day or the days to come to that household. Yet, ever and anon, in the midst of their joyousness, a strange look would leap from the quick, dark eyes of St. Victor, as he fixed them upon his sister's face, and an expression would flit across his own face inscrutable to the watchful physician. With a slight motion of his hand or head he would arrest and direct the doctor's attention, who would then perceive Miss Marchand's luminous glance changing into a look expressive of anxiety and terror, the glow of her cheeks fading into a pallor like that of one in a swoon. But, strange! an instant would change it all. The pallor, lingering but a moment, would melt away as a mist before the sun, and the roses would come back to the cheeks again in all their rosiness. The host would divert his companion's startled attention by gracefully pressing the viands upon his notice, or by some brilliant sally, so scintillating with wit or droll wisdom, as to have brought the smile to an anchorite's eyes.

"I pray you watch her! Did you not notice that slight incoherency?" he remarked, in a whisper, leaning over toward the doctor.

The doctor had noticed nothing but the playful badinage of a happy girl.

"I am afraid her loveliness blinds my judgment. I *must* see what there is in all this," he answered to himself, deprecatingly.

They sat long at table. Not that any one ate to excess, though the pompous English steward served up one delicious dish after another, including the time-honored Christmas feast requisite, — the plum-pudding, — which was tasted and approved, not to wound the Briton's national and professional vanity, but sent off, but slightly shorn of its proportions, to grace the servants' table.

The guest noticed that St. Victor partook very sparingly of food, although he fully enjoyed the occasion. Save tasting of the wild game and its condiment of real

Calcutta currie, he ate nothing of the leading dishes or *entrées*. Neither did he drink much wine, whose quality was of the rarest, being of his own stock drawn from his father's rich store in his Madeira cellar. Of the luscious grapes and oranges which formed a leading feature of the dessert, he partook more freely, as if they cooled his tongue. That there was fever, and nervous excitement, in the young man's frame, was evident. Indeed, to the doctor's observant eye, the brother appeared more delicate, and of a temperament more highly nervous than his sister.

The frankness, the almost childish confidence and open-heartedness of the young people formed one of their greatest attractions to the usually reticent, thoughtful physician. He felt his own impulses expanding under the warmth of their sunny natures until the very romance of his boyhood stirred again, and sprouted through the mould in which it lay dormant. There was nothing in their past history or present prospects which, seemingly, they cared to conceal, so that he had become possessed of a pretty fair history of their lives before the last course came upon the board. Both were born in the island of Madeira. St. Victor was twenty-four, Edith nineteen, years of age. Their mother was the daughter of an American merchant, long resident on the island ; their father was a French gentleman of fortune, who had retired to the island for his health, had loved and won the fair American girl, and lived with her a life of almost visionary beauty and happiness. Their father had joined their grandfather in some of his mercantile ventures; hence those voyages to the Indies, to South America, to the Mediterranean in which the children were participants. They also had spent a couple of years in France, cultivating the acquaintance of their relatives there, and adding some finishing touches to St. Victor's education, which, having been conducted under his father's eye by accomplished tutors, was unusually thorough and varied for one so young. This fact the doctor surmised during the progress of the banquet, though he did not ascertain the full extent of the young man's accomplishments until a future day. Nor was Edith's education overlooked. She was in a remarkable degree fitted to be the companion and confidante of her brother,—sympathizing in his tastes, reading his books, enjoying his pastimes, and sharing his ambitions to their utmost. It was a beautiful blending of natures,—such as the world too rarely beholds,—such as our received "systems" of education and association *cannot* produce.

Their grandfather had been dead for several years; their father for three, their mother for two. "She faded rapidly after father's death,—drooped like a frost-blighted flower," said St. Victor. "They had been too happy in this world to remain long apart in the next."

"You now see, doctor," the narrator of these family reminiscences at length said, "why Edith and myself are so unlike. My sister is her mother over again, fair and bright, like your New York ladies,—among the most beautiful women, in many respects, I have ever seen. I am dark and thin, — a very Frenchman in tastes, temperament, and habits."

He toyed a few moments with an orange; then, again leaning toward the physician, he said, in that sharp whisper which once before during the evening he had made use of, —

"I will tell you all, doctor. My father died insane. We afterwards learned that it was one of the inheritances of his haughty and wealthy family. The peace and delight which he had with his wife and children long delayed the terrible legacy; but it fell due at last. He died a maniac, — a raving maniac. *She* does not know it. It killed her mother. Imagine, doctor, *imagine*, if you can, how I watch over her! how I pity! how I dread! O God! to think that I must detect those symptoms, as I have done during the last six months. I have seen the virus in her eyes to-night. I have not breathed a word to her of my knowledge and convictions; but I am as certain of it as that she sits there. Look at her now, doctor, — *now!*" — with a stealthy side-glance at the beautiful girl who, at the moment, was smiling absently over a flower which she had taken from its vase, — smiling only as girls can, — as if it interpreted something deeper than a passing thought.

It is impossible to describe the strain of agony in the young man's voice; his sudden pallor; the sweat starting from his forehead; or to describe the piercing power of his eye, as he turned it from the face of his sister to that of his guest. Accustomed as he was to every form of suffering, Dr. Graham shrank from the appeal in that searching look, which mutely asked him if there were any hope.

The clear whisper in which St. Victor had spoken aroused Edith from her revery; she darted a glance at both parties, so full of suspicion and dread, so in contrast with her natural sunny expression, that it was as if her face had suddenly withered, from that of a child, to the thin features of the careworn woman of fifty. She half rose in her chair, faltered, sank back, and sat gazing fixedly at the two men; yet silent as a statue.

St. Victor was the first to recover himself. He burst into a light laugh, — sweet as a shower of flowers, — and, taking up a slender-necked decanter of pale wine, passed it to his guest, remarking, —

"We are forgetting that this is Christmas night. Fill your glass, my friend, with *this* wine, — the oldest and rarest of our precious store, — and I will fill mine. Then, we will both drink joyously to the health of my only darling — my one beloved — my sister."

He said this so prettily, poured out the wine with such arch pleasantry of gesture, that the color came back to Edith's cheeks; and when the two men bowed to her, before drinking, she gave them a smile, steeped in melancholy, but very sweet, and brimming with affection. It thrilled Dr. Graham's veins more warmly than the priceless wine.

"After our mother's death," continued St. Victor, in

his natural voice, "we found ourselves quite alone. We had formed no great attachment to our relatives in France; and, as one branch of our father's business remained still unsettled in this country, we resolved to come hither. Then, too, we had a longing to behold the land which was our mother's. When we had arranged and closed up our affairs in Madeira, we sailed for France, where we spent one winter only. I thought" — with a tender glance at his sister — "that a sea voyage would do Edith good. I was not satisfied about her health; so I drew her away from Paris, and, last spring, we fulfilled our promise to see our mother's land, and came hither. I am afraid the climate here does not agree with her. Do you think she looks well?"

The girl moved uneasily, casting a beseeching look at the speaker.

"It is not I who am not strong," she said; "it is you, St. Victor. If your friend is a doctor, I wish he would give a little examination into the state of your health. You are thin and nervous; you have no appetite, — while he can see, at a glance, that nothing in the world ails *me*."

Again her brother laughed; not gayly as before, but with a peculiar and subtle significance; while he gave the doctor another swift glance, saying to him in a low voice, —

"I have heard that persons threatened with certain mental afflictions never suspect their own danger."

Dr. Graham did not know if the young lady overheard

this remark; he glanced toward her, but her eyes again were upon the flowers, which she was pulling to pieces. He perceived that her lips trembled; but she still smiled, scattering the crimson leaves over the white clothes.

At this period of his novel visit, — just then and there, when St. Victor laughed that subtle laugh and his sister vacantly destroyed the red flower, — a conviction rushed into the physician's mind, or rather, we may say, pierced it through like a ray of light in a darkened room.

Instantly all was clear to him. From that moment he was cool and watchful, but so pained with this sudden knowledge of the true state of the case that he wished himself well out of that splendid house, back in his own dreary office. He wished himself away, because he already loved these young people, and his sympathy with them was too keen to allow him further to enjoy himself; yet, in all his medical experience, he had never been so interested with a professional interest. As a physician, he felt a keen pleasure; as a friend, a keen pain. His faculties each sprang to its post, awaiting the next development of the scene.

While Mr. Marchand was giving some order to his steward, the beautiful girl at his other hand leaned toward him, and also whispered confidentially in his ear: "Dr. Graham, if you really are my brother's friend, I pray you watch him closely, and tell me at some future time if you have any fears — any suspicions of — Oh, I implore you, sir, do not deceive me!"

Her eyes were filled with tears, her voice choked.

The thing was absurd. Its ludicrous aspect struck the listener, almost forcing him to laugh; while the tears, at the same time, arose responsive in his own eyes.

A clock on the mantel chimed nine. The steward placed on the board the last delicacies of the feast, — Neapolitan creams and orange-water ice.

"Edith chooses luscious things like creams," remarked her brother. "Which will you have, doctor? As for me, I prefer ices; they cool my warm blood, which is fierce like tropic air. Ah, this is delicious! I am feverish, I believe; and the scent of the orange brings back visions of our dear island home."

He paused, as if his mind were again on the vine-clad hills of the "blessed isle." Then he spoke, suddenly, —

"Edith, have some of this?"

She smiled, shaking her head.

"But you *must.* I insist. You need it. Don't you agree with me, doctor, that it is just what she requires?"

He spoke in a rising key, with a rapid accent. Edith reached forth her hand, and took the little dish of orange ice. It shook like a lily in the wind; but she said, softly and with apparent calmness, —

"Anything to please you, brother. I will choose this every day if you think it good for me."

He gave her a satisfied look. Then there was a brief silence, which their guest was about to dissipate with a playful remark, when St. Victor turned abruptly to the steward, —

"Thompson," he cried, "now bring in the skeleton!"

"What, sir?" stammered the astonished servant.

"Bring in the skeleton, I said. Do you not know that the Egyptians always crown their feasts with a death's head? Bring it in, I say, and place it — *there!*"

Half-rising in his seat, he pointed to the vacant space behind his sister's chair.

The man now smiled, thinking his master jested; but his expression grew more questioning and anxious as the bright eyes turned upon him glittering in anger.

"Why am I not obeyed? Bring in the skeleton, I repeat, and place it behind my sister's chair. It is in the house; you will have no difficulty in finding it. It has lurked here long. I have been aware of its presence these many months, — always following, following my dear Edith, — a shadow in her steps. You see how young and fair she is; but it is all hollow — ashes — coffin-dust! She does not know of it; she has never even turned her head when it lurked behind her; but to-night she must make its acquaintance. It will not longer be put off. Our feast is nearly over. Bring it in, Thompson, and we will salute it."

The steward, with a puzzled look, turned from one to another of the company. Miss Marchand had risen to her feet, and was regarding her brother with terrified eyes, stretching out her hands toward him. The doctor, too, arose, not in excitement, but with commingled pain and resolution stamped upon his features; while his gaze rested upon the face of St. Victor until the eyes of the young man were riveted and arrested by the doctor's demeanor. A flush then diffused itself gradually over Marchand's pale countenance; his thin nostrils quivered; his fingers twitched and trembled and sought his bosom, as if in search of something concealed there. Then he laughed once more that short, nervous laugh so significant to the physician's ears, and cried, in a high tone,—

"So, Edith, you did not know that you were going mad? *I* did. I've watched you night and day this long time. I have all along been afraid it would end as it has — on Christmas night. *That* was the day our father tried to murder our mother. An anniversary, then, we have to-night celebrated. Ha, ha! And you didn't know the skeleton was awaiting admittance to the banquet!"

His eyes gleamed with a light at once of delight and with malice; but he quietly added,—

"But *I* shall not harm you, you demented thing, you beautiful insanity. There! doctor, didn't I tell you to watch her — to read her — to comprehend the subtle thing? So full of art and duplicity! But look at her now — *now!* She is as mad as the serpent which has poisoned itself with its own fangs — mad — mad! O God! has it come to this? But, I knew it — knew the skeleton was her skeleton — the bones without her beautiful flesh. We've had enough of it now. Take it away, Thompson, — hurry it away!"

"Appear to obey him. Pretend that you take something from the room," said Dr. Graham, in an undertone, to the servant, while St. Victor's eyes were fixed glaring and lurid upon his trembling, agonized, speechless sister.

The skeleton had, in truth, appeared at the Christmas feast.

Laying his hand firmly upon the young man's wrist the doctor said, —

"Mr. Marchand, you're not well, to-night. You are over-fatigued. Shall we go upstairs?"

St. Victor's quickly flashing gaze was met by that clear, resolute, almost fierce response in the physician's eye, before which he hesitated, then shrank. The madman had his master before him.

"You are right. I am not very well; my head aches; I'm worn out with this trouble about Edith, doctor. *Do* you think it is hopeless? She had better come with us. I don't like to leave her alone with that hideous shape at her back."

Obeying the gentle but firm pull upon his wrist, the brother turned to leave the room, looking back wistfully upon his sister. She was following them with clasped hands, and a face from which all youth and color had fled. St. Victor suddenly paused, gave a scream like the cry of a panther, wrenched himself quickly from the grasp upon his arm, and, in an instant, his teeth were buried in the white shoulder of his sister. But only for an instant, for almost as quickly as the madman's movement had been the doctor's. One terrible blow of his fist sent the maniac to the floor like a clod.

"O doctor! why did you do it?"

"To save your life, Miss Marchand."

"Poor St. Victor! His fate is on him at last."

Her voice was calm in its very despair. She sank down beside the senseless man, lifting the worn, white face to her lap and covering it with kisses. "I saw it, —yet I did not think it would come so soon. O God! be pitiful! Have I not prayed enough?"

The lips of the injured man began to quiver. "We must bind him and get him to bed before he fully recovers," said the doctor, lifting Edith to her feet. "Here, Thompson, help me to carry him to his bed."

When the maniac recovered consciousness fully, his ravings were fearful. It was the malady of frenzy in its most appalling condition. The extent of the mental wreck Dr. Graham had, for the last half hour of the feast, been trying to fathom. When he dealt that dreadful blow he knew the wreck was complete: reason had gone out forever with that panther-like shriek. All that could be done was to secure the maniac against injury to himself or others, and to administer such anti-spasmodics or anæsthetics as, in some degree, would control the paroxysms.

Poor St. Victor! So young, so gifted, so blest with

worldly goods; his fate was upon him, as Edith had said.

From that hour he had but brief respite from torment. Not a gleam of sanity came from those fiery eyes; all was fierce, untamable, inhuman, as if the life had been one of storm and crime, instead of peace and purity. Did there lay upon that racking bed a proof of the natural depravity of the creature man, when the creature was uncontrolled by a reasoning, responsible will? Or, was it not rather a proof that the mental machine was in disorder, by a distention of the blood-vessels and their engorgement in the brain,—that cerebral excitement was a purely physical phenomenon, dependent upon simple, physical causes, which science some day shall define and skill shall counteract?

Happily, the fire in the sufferer's brain scorched and consumed the sources of his life, as flames drink up the water that is powerless to quench them. Day by day he wasted; and, in less than a month from that night,—Christmas evening,—St. Victor Marchand's form was at peace in death.

During all that time Dr. Graham never left the sufferer's bedside. Day and night he was there at his post, doing all that was possible to alleviate the pain. The skill of a physician and the love of a brother were exhausted in that battle with death in its most dreaded form.

His care was, too, required for Miss Edith. Her life was so interwoven with that of her brother, that the doctor doubted if she could survive the shock to her sympathies and affection. When the surprise of the tragedy was over, on the day following the first outburst of the malady, she told him that for months she had feared the worst. She had remarked symptoms so like her father's as to excite her fears; yet, with the happiness of youth, the sister persuaded herself that her apprehensions were groundless. His sunny nature seemed proof against the approach of an evil so blasting; and her momentary fears were banished by the very mood of heightened vivacity and excitement which had awakened them. Having no intimate friend in whom to confide, none to counsel, she had borne the weight of her inward sorrow and dread alone.

At intervals, during Christmas day, she had observed an incoherency in her brother's speech, and an unwonted nervousness of manner, which had inspired her with serious alarm. When he proposed to drive out, she encouraged the suggestion, hoping that the cold air might restore him to his usual state. Upon his return with Dr. Graham, he had seemed so entirely like himself, so happy, so disposed to enjoyment, that she once more dismissed every thought of danger, until she overheard the sharp whispers in which he addressed his guest.

"And oh, to think," she cried, while the tears rained down her cheeks, "that in his love for me, his madness should take the shape of beholding the conditions of his own brain reflected in mine! He was so afraid harm would come to me, — thoughtful of me so long as even the shadow of sanity remained. Dear, dear St. Victor, — so good, so pure, so wise! Why was not *I* the victim, if it was fated that there must be one?" Then lifting her tearful eyes, — "Doctor, perhaps the poison lurks in my veins, too! Tell me, do you think there is danger that I, too, shall one day go mad?"

"No, poor child, most emphatically, I do *not*. You must not permit such a fancy to enter your mind. As St. Victor said, you are your mother's image and counterpart, in temperament and mental quality, while he, doubtless, in all active or positive elements of constitution and temperament, was his father's reflex. Is it not true?"

"I believe so. My dear father used, I know, to think St. Victor nearer to him than I could be. When together, they looked and acted very much alike. Poor, dear brother!" and again the tears coursed down her cheeks.

The doctor was deeply moved; this grief was so inexpressibly deep as to stir in his heart every emotion of tenderness and sympathy it was possible for a gentle-souled man to feel.

"I loved him," he said, gently, "before I had known him an hour. His nature was like a magnet, to draw love. Alas! it is sad, when the promise of such a life is blighted. I would have given my life for his, could it have averted this terrible blow from this house."

A radiant, soul-full look dwelt in her tear-dimmed eyes. That this man — a comparative stranger — should manifest this interest in her brother aroused all the gratitude and affection of her warm nature.

"And I love you, Dr. Graham, for loving him," she said, in the pathos of the language that never speaks untruthfully,—the pathos of irrepressible feeling. Then she added: "Do not leave us, doctor. You are all the friend we have here in this great city. If you leave us I shall, indeed, be alone."

"I will remain, my dear child, so long as there is need of my services."

He did not tell her, in so many words, that the case was hopeless; but her eye was quick to see the wasting form and the growing prostration which followed each paroxysm. How those two faithful attendants watched and waited for the end! And in the grief for the sister, the physician's gentleness found that road to a mutual devotion, which is sure to open before those who love and wait upon a common object of affection. The doctor and sister became, without a consciousness of their real feeling, mutually dependent and trusting.

In less than a month, as we have written, the skeleton which came to the feast on Christmas night departed from the house to abide on St. Victor Marchand's grave.

At the next meeting of the Institute, Doctor Graham gave a full account of the case, remarking upon the singular feature in it of the madness assuming an embodiment in the sanity of another. From much that Edith told him, as well as from his own observation and knowledge, he was convinced that, for months, the young man had detected every minute symptom and development of his disease in his sister; and had a physician been at hand, he could have traced the insidious progress of the malady in the strength of the brother's suspicions regarding his sister. The facts cited to the Institute touched the compassion of the most practice-hardened physician when Dr. Graham related the strange and pitying tenderness with which young Marchand had watched his sister, and strove to divert from her mind the madness which tainted his blood alone.

"Alone in this great city. If you leave me, I shall be alone indeed." The words were like an angel's rap upon the heart's door. In his own great trouble, — the loss of his wife, — the physician deemed himself afflicted beyond his deserts; but what was his condition compared with that of this youthful, tender, dependent woman, whose loss isolated her from all others?

No, not all others. After the first black cloud of her sorrow had drifted away, she turned to him, whose hand had sustained her, even when prayer had left her helpless and hopeless, — turned to him with a love that was more than a love, with an adoration, before which the physician bent, in wonder and satisfaction. He drew her to his bosom as something to be kept with all the truth and tenderness of an abiding love.

The dull office has been exchanged for a home that is like a palace of dreams; and Edith Graham, never forgetting her great sorrow, yet became one of the happiest of all who ever loved.

LET THOSE LAUGH WHO WIN.

LET THOSE LAUGH WHO WIN.

MR. PONTIFEX POMPADOUR was a gentleman whose family record testified to his having breathed the breath of life sixty years, and yet his appearance bore witness to not more than forty. Appearances, however, though they are deceitful, result from causes more or less palpable; and, in this case, they could be naturally accounted for.

Ecce testem!

Mr. Pompadour's complexion was clear and transparent,—but it was not his own. His teeth were white and regular,—but they were artificial. His hair was black and glossy,—but it was dyed. His whiskers were ibid.,—but they were ditto. His dress was the perfection of fashion and taste, though rather youthful; and withal he carried himself with a jaunty air, and a light and springing step, smiling blandly on all he met, as if smiles were dollars and he were dispensing them right royally.

He had an only son,—Augustus Fitz Clarence Pompadour,—who was heir-apparent to the very considerable property supposed to belong to the "said aforesaid." This son was twenty-three, and had graduated at college with some knowledge of some things, if not of some others. He was a modern Mithridates in his power to withstand strychnine and nicotine; and he had devoted much attention to that branch of geometry which treats of the angles of balls on a cushion. One beautiful trait in his character, however, was his tender affection for his father, which showed itself most touchingly — whenever he was in need of money.

In person he was prepossessing, having light-blue eyes, dark-brown hair, and a drooping moustache. Nor will I allow that he was a vicious lad. Indolent and useless he certainly was, — an insignificant numeral in the great sum of humanity, but a *roué* he certainly was not. The worst thing about him was his name, and that he received from a weak, silly novel-reading mother, who gave her life for his, and, with her dying breath, charged his father to pay this homage to the yellow-covered world in which she had lived.

If there was anything wanting in the comfortable mansion, where the Pompadours, father and son, kept bachelor's hall, it was the refining and softening influence of woman. And this brings us to the consideration of the skeleton which abode in the closets of Pompadour and son.

The late Mrs. Pompadour had possessed some property which she had retained after marriage. Before her death she made a will, leaving to Augustus the fee, and to his father the income of the estate. In case, however, Augustus should marry before his father *did*, he was to enter into full possession of the property. Wives, in dying, do not generally offer their husbands a premium for replacing them; and so the judges inferred that the real meaning of the testatrix would be arrived at by inserting the letter *e* in the word "*did;*" thus making the contingency turn upon Augustus' marrying before his father *died.* Moreover, the lawyer who drew the will (his ancestor was limned by Æsop in the fable of the Ass in the lion's skin) swore positively to this rendering being in accordance with the wish of the deceased, and so the courts decided that in the event of Mr. Pompadour's marrying before his son, he should retain his interest during life.

Now Mr. Pompadour, aside from mercenary motives, was very uxoriously inclined; and would doubtless have married years before, had he not set too high an estimate on himself.

His condition of mind at the beginning of this history might be expressed logically somewhat as follows: —

First, he must get married.

Second, Augustus must *not.*

And Augustus, by analogous reasoning on identical premises, *mutatis mutandis*, had arrived at a dual conclusion.

First, he must get married.

Second, his father must *not.*

A vigorous system of espionage had been instituted by father and son, on the actions of each other. Skirmishes had been frequent; and if neither gained any decided advantage, neither lost. But the great battle of the war was yet to be fought, and it has been reserved for my pen to inscribe its history.

In the suburban village where Mr. Pompadour resided was a handsome residence; and its owner, "about visiting Europe," offered it for rent. The house was elegant, and the grounds especially fine. They were flanked by two shady streets and fronted on a third. A widow lady with one daughter became the tenant; and, as is usual in such cases, the whole village called upon her,— three persons prompted by politeness, and three hundred by curiosity. The cards which did duty for the lady in returning these calls, announced her to be "Mrs. Telluria Taragon, *née* Trelauney." By the same token her daughter was discovered to be "Miss Terpsichore Taragon."

Mrs. Taragon was one of the most bewitching of widows. About forty (she acknowledged to thirty-three), she was the very incarnation of matronly beauty. She was just tall enough to be graceful, and just plump enough not to be unwieldy. Her eyes were black and dangerous. Her hair was short, and it clustered over her forehead in little ringlets,—rather girlish, but very becoming. Her teeth were white and natural, and she had a most fascinating smile, which showed her teeth in a carefully unstudied manner, formed a pretty dimple in her chin, and enabled her to look archly without apparent intention.

Her daughter, Miss Terpsichore, was twenty, with a slender, graceful form, and a pair of rosy cheeks, before whose downy softness the old simile of the peach becomes wholly inadequate. She had hazel eyes, whose liquid depths reflected the brightest and sunniest of tempers, and dark brown hair, with just a suspicion of golden shimmer filtering through its wavy folds.

Mrs. Taragon, on the bare charge, could not have escaped conviction as a "designing widow." She not only was on the lookout, perpetually, for an investment of her daughter, but she was flying continually from her cap a white flag of unconditional surrender to the first man bold enough to attack herself.

Mr. Pontifex Pompadour "availed himself of an early opportunity" to call upon Mrs. Taragon. His fame had preceded him; and that estimable lady, who was in her boudoir when he was announced, gave a small shriek of dismay at her dishevelled appearance. However, no one need be alarmed at such a manifestation on the part of a "lady of fashion." It is indicative of perfect satisfaction with her general effect. Mrs. Taragon flew to her mirror to shake out another curl — and her flounces; smiled bewitchingly by way of rehearsal; bit her lips frantically to bring the blood *to* them, and walked aimlessly about the room for a few moments with her hands above her head, to send the blood *out* of them. Then picking up her handkerchief daintily, and going downstairs slowly, that her cheeks might not be too much flushed, she acquired sudden animation at the parlor-door, and burst into the room with an elaborate rustle, and a thousand apologies for having kept Mr. Pompadour waiting so long,—and wasn't "the day perfectly lovely?"

If a conversation be interesting, or serve in any way to develop the plot of a story, I hold that it should be given at full length; but the polite nothings which were repeated at *this* interview, came under neither of these heads. They served only to display Mr. Pompadour's false teeth, and Mrs. Taragon's real ones (and the dimple) through the medium of Mr. P.'s real smile and Mrs. T.'s false one.

The two parted mutually pleased, and Mrs. Taragon said to herself, as she resumed the novel she had dropped at Mr. Pompadour's entrance, "If I marry *him*, I will have that set of sables, and those diamonds I saw at Tiffany's."

Mr. Pompadour beheaded a moss rose with his cane, as he stepped jauntily down the walk, and remarked to his inner self, "A monstrous fine woman that, and I may say, without vanity, that she was struck with my appearance. Why, ho! who the devil's that?"

The acute reader will perceive a slight incoherence in the latter portion of this remark. It was due to a sight which met Mr. Pompadour's gaze on stepping into the street from Mrs. Taragon's domain. This was nothing else than Augustus Fitz Clarence walking leisurely up the street with a young lady whom we know — but the illustrious parent did not — to be Miss Terpsichore Taragon.

"Confound the boy!" said the old gentleman, "I wonder who he's got there? Just like his father, though! For I may say, without vanity, that I was a tremendous fellow among the girls."

Augustus Fitz Clarence was not at all pleased at this chance rencontre. The intimacy with the charming widow, which it strongly hinted at, brought vividly to his mind its possible results upon his own prospects. And, moreover, he was conscious of a peculiar and novel sensation in regard to the young lady, which made him rather shamefaced under the paternal eye. In short, he was in love. All the symptoms were apparent: a rush of blood to the face, and a stammering in the speech, whenever proximity to the infecting object induced a spasm. He also had the secondary symptoms, — a sensation of the spinal cord, as if molasses were being poured down the back, and a general feeling "all over," such as little boys call "goose-flesh," and which is ordinarily occasioned by a ghost story, or a cold draught from an open doorway.

To the writer, who stands upon the high level of the philosophic historian, it is evident that the same feelings warmed the gentle breast of Terpsichore that burned in the bosom of Augustus. To furnish food, however, for the unextinguishable laughter of the gods, this fact is never made clear to the principals themselves till the last moment. "And so from hour to hour we ripe and ripe . . . . and thereby hangs a tale."

With the foregoing paragraph, I bridge over an "hiatus, as it were," of several months.

Respect for truth obliges me to record the fact, that Mrs. Taragon regarded her daughter with that unchristian feeling called jealousy. But, if a heartless, she was a shrewd woman, and she meant to dispose of Terpsichore advantageously.

There was, at this time, and I believe there is still, in the village of which I write, an "order of the garter," under the control of one Mrs. Grundy, the motto of which was: "Those are evil of whom we evil speak." Its evening meetings were familiarly known as the "nights of the sewing-circle;" and it was the duty of each member to attend to everybody's business but his own. An agent of this order promptly put Mrs. Taragon in possession of everything which had been discovered or invented concerning Mr. Pompadour, not forgetting to enlarge upon the conditions of the will. Mrs. Taragon thereupon resolved to marry Mr. Pompadour; for, in addition to other reasons, she confessed to herself that she really liked him. As may be supposed, therefore, she looked with much disfavor on the increasing intimacy between the young people; but she feared that any violent attempt to rupture it would precipitate the very result she would avoid. She sat, one day, in a brown study, regarding the subject in all its bearings, with her comely cheek resting upon her plump hand, and, at last, arrived at a conclusion.

"I think it would not be wise," she said, consulting the mirror to see if her hand had left any mark upon her cheek, — "to interfere just at present; at any rate, not till I am *sure* of Mr. Pompadour; but I will keep a close watch upon them."

Not many days afterwards, a picturesque group occupied the bow-window of Mrs. Taragon's drawing-room. Mrs. T. herself, quite covered with an eruption of worsted measles, was the principal figure. At her feet, like Paul at Gamaliel's, sat Augustus; but, unlike Paul, he held a skein of worsted. Nestling on an ottoman in the recess of the window was Terpsichore, inventing floral phenomena in water-colors, and looking very bewitching.

"'Twas a fair scene." As under the shade of some far-spreading oak, when noon holds high revel in the heavens, the gentle flock cluster in happy security, fearing no dire irruption of lupine enemy, so --

"Mr. Pompadour," announced the servant.

"The devil!" echoed Augustus Fitz Clarence.

Mrs. Taragon's first impulse was to spring up and greet her visitor cordially. Her second, to do no such thing. Napoleon said, "An opportunity lost is an occasion for misfortune." Here was her Austerlitz or her Waterloo! With the rapidity of genius, she laid the plot for a little comedy of "The Jealous Lovers," to the success of which the actors themselves unwittingly contributed.

Half rising, she acknowledged Mr. Pompadour's elaborate bow, and, motioning him gracefully to a seat, sank back into her chair. Then, pretending that the worsted was knotted, she bent her curls so near Augustus' face, and made a whispered remark with such a conscious air, that the blood rushed to that young man's face in an instant.

"I saw you out riding yesterday, Mr. Pompadour," said the cheerful widow, pleased that her first shot had taken effect. "And what a *beautiful* horse! and you ride *so* gracefully!"

"Thank you, madam," said Mr. Pompadour, stiffly; "I think I may say, without vanity, that I do ride tolerably well."

"And you," to the son, "now your father is present, I must call you *Mr.* Augustus, — may I not?" she said, coaxingly. The "Mr." was emphasized, as if when alone she did not use it. But this was, of course, unintentional.

Now Augustus, for some time, had endeavored to ingratiate himself with Mrs. Taragon, but with little success, and, therefore, he was utterly unable to comprehend her sudden benignity. He glanced at his father, and met the eyes of that individual glaring on him with the look of an ogre deprived of his baby lunch. He glanced at Terpsichore, but that young lady was absorbed with a new discovery in botany. He glanced at Mrs. Taragon, but she was calmly winding worsted.

"Terpy, dear," said her mother, "*do* show Mr. Pompadour some of your drawings. My dear little girl is *so* devoted to art!" she exclaimed, enthusiastically, as the daughter rose to bring her portfolio. "Take care, Mr. Augustus; you know worsted is a dreadful thing to snarl." Augustus had involuntarily sprung up to offer his assistance, but he sank back in confusion.

"Are you fond of engravings, Mr. Pompadour?" asked the young lady, sweetly.

"Ah! yes! I—I think I may say without vanity,"—began Mr. Pompadour, but he finished silently to himself,—"D— me, I'll make her jealous!" Whose Austerlitz or Waterloo should it be? He put on his eye-glass to inspect the volume, and for a little while almost forgot his egotism in admiration of the beauty of nature beside him, if not of the beauties of art before him.

Augustus was not slow in perceiving that, for some unknown reason, Mrs. Taragon's attention was gained, and he tried desperately to improve the occasion. Every once in a while, however, his eyes would wander toward his father, who played his part with so much skill that the bosom of Augustus was soon filled with burnings, and the mind of the widow with perplexities. The gentle heart of Terpsichore was grieved also, and her mind sorely puzzled at the enigmatical conduct of those about her, while she was somewhat annoyed at the pertinacious attentions of the elder P.

The distinguished gentleman who wrote so graphically about the "Elbows of the Mincio," must confess that *our* Quadrilateral is only second to that which he has helped to embalm in history. The Irishman's experience with the large boot and the small one, and the other pair similarly mismated, was here reproduced with painful reality. Some evil genius had scattered wormwood on the air, and asphyxia, or something worse, seemed likely to supervene, when the entrance of another visitor broke the charm, and the *tête-à-tête*, and the gentlemen fled.

The thermometer of Mr. Pompadour's temper indicated boiling heat. He sputtered and fumed like an irascible old gentleman as he was, and managed to work himself into a crazy fit of jealousy, about his son and the too fascinating widow ; and, oddly enough, this feeling thus aroused by the green-eyed monster, for the time being, quite eclipsed his mercenary muddle. So, upon poor Augustus, as the available subject, fell palpable and uncomfortable demonstrations of paternal displeasure.

For several days Mr. Pompadour stayed away from Mrs. Taragon's, and that good lady began to fear lest she had overdrawn her account at the bank of his heart, and that further drafts would be dishonored. The thought of such a catastrophe was torture of the most refined quality. By an illogical system of reasoning, peculiar to the female mind, she imagined that Terpsichore was the cause of his desertion, and that young lady thereupon became the recipient of an amount of small spite and aggravated vindictiveness, which reflected great credit upon Mrs. Taragon's inquisitorial capabilities.

She had, it must be obvious, set her heart upon having those diamonds from Tiffany's.

At the end of a week, however, Mr. Pompadour called upon Mrs. Taragon, and this time he found her alone. His countenance gave proof of some desperate resolution. His attire was more than usually elegant. His hair and whiskers were a trifle blacker and glossier than ever. He had a rose in his button-hole, and yellow kids on his hands. Solomon, in all his glory, was not arrayed (I sincerely trust) like unto him! Mrs. Taragon rose cordially, and held out to him her plump little hand; it lay a moment in his, as if asking to be squeezed. Mr. Pompadour looked as if he would like to squeeze it, and perhaps he did.

The lady's cordiality soon gave place to a timid shyness. To use a military phrase, she was "feigning a retreat." Mr. Pompadour waxed bold and advanced. The conversation skirmished awhile, the widow occasionally making a sally, and driving in the enemy's outposts, his main body meanwhile steadily approaching. The tone in which they conducted hostilities, however, gradually fell, and if one had been near enough he might have heard Mr. Pompadour remark, with a kind of quiet satisfaction, "For I think I may say, without vanity, I still possess some claim to good looks." The widow's reply was so low that our reporter failed to catch it, and then — military phraseology avaunt! — the old veteran knelt on the carpet, and surrendered at discretion.

"Good gracious, Mr. Pompadour!" exclaimed the

widow, with well-feigned alarm, at the same time picking a thread off her dress, "*Do* get up, somebody may come in!"

"Never!" said the old hero stoutly, seeing his advantage, and determined to have its full benefit, "at any rate, not till you promise to marry me!"

A form passed the window. This time Mrs. Taragon was really frightened. "I will," she said hurriedly; "now get up, and sit down."

Mr. Pompadour leaped to his feet with the agility of a boy — of sixty, and imprinted a kiss lovingly upon the lady's nose, there not being time to capture the right place on the first assault. What followed we will leave to the imagination of the reader.

It was now October, and the trees had adorned themselves in their myriad dyes. The maple had put on crimson, the hickory a rich gold, and the oak a deep scarlet; while the pine and the hemlock "mingled with brighter tints the living green."

To the woods one balmy day Augustus and Terpsichore went together, to gather leaves for wreaths and screens. Both were carelessly happy, and the pines echoed their merry voices as they laughed and sang. At length the basket, which Augustus carried, was filled with gorgeous booty, and they sat down upon a fallen log, while Terpsichore wove a garland for her hair. No wonder that in the tranquil beauty of the scene their noisy mirth should become hushed. No wonder that, as the sun stole through the branches, and like Jove of old fell in a shower of gold about them, upon both their hearts fell the perfect peace of love! With the full tide of this feeling came to Augustus the resolve to know his fate; for he felt that upon that answer hung his destiny.

They sat in silence while he tried to teach his tongue the language of his heart. Then he glanced timidly at the maiden, but her head was drooped low over the wreath, and her cheeks reflected its crimson dye.

"Miss Taragon," he said, at length, abruptly, "were you ever in love?"

She started like a frightened bird. The rich blood fled to her heart, and left her face pallid as marble.

"I—I—don't know," she stammered. "Why do you ask me such a question?"

"Because," he said, "then you may know how I feel, and pity me! O Terpsichore!" he added passionately, "I love you with my whole soul, and if you will but bless me with your love, my whole life shall be devoted to your happiness."

And so he talked on in an impetuous strain, of mingled prayer and protestation, which was stereotyped long before the invention of printing.

Terpsichore's heart beat wildly. The color came and went in her cheeks, and she turned her head away to conceal her emotion.

The wreath lay finished in her lap; and at last, with a bright smile, she placed it on his forehead; and, clasping his hand in both her own, she kissed him on the forehead. And now we might as well leave them alone together.

Mrs. Taragon, having made sure of Mr. Pompadour, now proceeded to carry out her plan of throwing obstacles in the way of the young people. Augustus, of course, was not aware of her complete information in regard to his "property qualifications," and attributed her disfavor to personal dislike. Whatever her motives, however, her actions were unequivocal; and Terpsichore, especially, had a sorry time of it. So uncomfortable did matters become, that, upon a review of the situation, and an eloquent appeal from Augustus, she consented to take with him that irrevocable step, to which Virgil undoubtedly alluded under the fine figure of "Descensus Averni." In plain English, they resolved to run away and be married.

I will not weary the reader with details of the preliminaries. They are unimportant to my narrative. A note, dispatched by Augustus to the Rev. Ebenezer Fiscuel, informed that gentleman that about half-past ten o'clock of an appointed evening he would be waited on by a couple desirous of being united in holy matrimony.

Augustus arranged to have a carriage in waiting under Terpsichore's window about ten o'clock, and, with the aid of a ladder and the above-mentioned clergyman, he hoped to settle the vexed question of the property, and render all further opposition to their union of an *ex post facto* character.

The evening came, and it found Mrs. Taragon and her daughter seated together in the parlor. Terpsichore was crocheting a net, which, like Penelope's, grew very slowly. She was nervous and fidgety. Her eyes wandered restlessly from her mother to the door, and she started at the slightest sound. Mrs. Taragon seemed uncommonly suspicious and alert. She was reading, but had not turned a leaf for half an hour. She glanced furtively and continually about the room.

"She has found us out," thought Terpsichore, and her heart almost stopped beating. With a great effort she controlled herself, and had recourse to stratagem.

"Mother, dear," she said, dropping the net in her lap, "you look tired; why don't you go to bed?"

"Oh, no, darling," said the widow, cheerfully, "I don't feel a bit weary. But your eyes look red, and I think *you* had better retire."

"No, mamma, not yet," she replied. "I want to finish this net. I have done so little upon it lately."

A slight shade of vexation crossed the face of the widow.

"If you had devoted yourself to the net," she said, spitefully, "it would have been finished."

Terpsichore blushed guiltily. Augustus had spent more than two hours with her that day; and she felt a presentiment that impending wrath was about to descend on her devoted head.

"I am sure, mother," she said, quietly, "*you* can't complain of my seeing too much company."

This shot told; for Mr. Pompadour had been very attentive of late.

Mrs. Taragon nearly tore a leaf out of her book.

"At any rate," she retorted, "my visitors are respectable."

Terpsichore's lip quivered. The remark was cruel, but it roused her spirit.

"If my company is not respectable," she said, with an incipient sob, "it is the fault of his bringing up."

Mr. Pompadour was hit this time, right between his eyes. The widow blazed.

"You — you — you minx," she said, angrily, "I believe you'd like to see me dead, and out of your way!"

The remark was utterly irrelevant; but she saw it in the book, and thought it would be dramatic.

Terpsichore burst into tears, and beat a retreat in disorder. As she left the room, Mrs. Taragon said to herself, with a sigh of relief, —

"Well, the coast is clear for Pompadour, — and she's safe for to-night, any way."

Which was a slight mistake.

"Ten o'clock came, and with it the carriage. A man glided silently underneath Terpsichore's window, and a ladder was reared against the wall. Silently the window opened, and a form descended the ladder, and was clasped in an equally silent embrace at the foot. Terpsichore had not entirely recovered her spirits, but she stifled her emotions for the sake of Augustus. For the same reason she did not scold him for rumpling her bonnet. Hurrying into the carriage, they drove rapidly away.

As they turned the corner into the principal street, another carriage, going in the same direction, came up behind them at a quick trot. Augustus sprang to his feet, and peered out into the darkness. "Betrayed," was the thought which flashed through his mind, and he muttered an eighteen-cornered oath. Terpsichore clung to his coat with an energy which indirectly reflected lasting credit upon his tailor.

"Put on more steam," whispered Augustus hoarsely to the driver, and the horses dashed onward at a breakneck pace, soon leaving the other carriage far behind.

At the rate they were going, it took but a few minutes to reach the parsonage. Directing the coachman to drive round the corner and wait, Augustus half-led, half-carried the trembling girl into the house. The Rev. Fiscuel's family and one or two neighbors were assembled in the parlor. The ceremony was soon performed, and an earnest blessing invoked upon the married life of the young people. As they were receiving the congratulations suited to the occasion, a juvenile Fiscuel came in, and whispered something to his father. Mr. Fiscuel, with a smile, turned to Augustus, saying, "My son tells me that your father is coming in at the gate with a lady."

The newly-married looked at each other in mute surprise. "I'll bet a hat," exclaimed Augustus, suddenly, "it's your mother; and they've come to get married!"

The Rev. Ebenezer spoke eagerly: "Did you send me two messages this morning?"

"No!" said Augustus; "of course I did not."

"Then they have, verily," exclaimed the clergyman, in a tone of very unclerical excitement; "for I received two messages from 'Mr. Pompadour.' I spoke of the singularity at the time."

"Can you hide us somewhere?" said Augustus, "till you've 'done' the old gentleman?"

"Come in here," said Mrs. Fiscuel, who had her share of that leaven of unrighteousness which is usually called fun. As she spoke, she opened the drawing-room door.

The Rev. Ebenezer sat down to write a certificate for Augustus; and, as one door closed upon the young couple, the other opened to admit the older one. If not in as great a hurry as their children, they seemed equally desirous of making assurance doubly sure. The family and the witnesses, who had followed Mrs. Fiscuel out of the apartment, were again summoned, and, for a second time that evening, the words were spoken which made a Pompadour and a Taragon "one bone and one flesh." Watching the proceedings through the crevice of the half-opened door, was a couple not counted among the "witnesses," and certainly not invited by the principals.

When the ceremony was over, Augustus and Terpsichore entered the room. Their appearance created what "Jenkins" would call "a profound sensation." Mr. Pompadour looked bowie-knives and six-shooters. Mrs. P., darning-needles and stilettoes. Augustus was self-possessed. Perhaps he remembered the old saying, "Let those laugh who win."

"We happened here not knowing you were coming," he said, addressing both; "wont you accept our congratulations."

Suddenly Mrs. Pompadour *née* Trelawney, gave a scream, and fell back in a chair, with symptoms of hysterics. She had caught sight of the *ring* on her daughter's finger, and comprehended everything in an instant,—the carriage which had fled before them as they left the house; this "accidental" visit to the minister's; and, worse than all, how she had been outwitted!

Terpsichore sprang forward to assist her.

"Go away from me! Go away! Don't let her touch me!" she screamed, throwing her arms about like a wind-mill. "I wont have it! I wont! I wont!"

Mr. Pompadour, during this outburst, showed signs of exasperation; apparently, however, he did not see the point, but was fast concluding that he had married a lunatic.

Terpsichore was frightened and began to cry. Augustus, to reässure her, put his arm around her waist. At this, the senior Mrs. Pompadour sprang up, and seized her husband by the arm, so energetically that it made him wince. Pointing to the tell-tale ring with a gesture worthy of Ristori, she managed to articulate: "Don't you see it? That undutiful girl has married Augustus, and — and he has married *her!*

Mr. Pompadour "saw it," and uttered some words which were not a blessing.

THE PROPER USE OF GRANDFATHERS.

THE PROPER USE OF GRANDFATHERS.

IF people without grandfathers are in need of any particular solace, they may find it in the fact that those cumbrous contingencies of existence cannot be continually stuck in their faces. A wise man has remarked, that the moderns are pigmies standing upon the shoulders of giants. He would have been wiser still, had he observed how frequently the giants change places with the pigmies, and ride them to death like Old Men of the Sea. If, at sixteen, I have the dyspepsia and a tendency to reflect on the problems of my being, I am begged to notice that, at a corresponding period old Jones, of the alternate generation, was gambolling o'er the dewy meads, a gleesome boy. If my baby cries and is puny at teething-time, the oracles, with an intuitive perception how my grandfather behaved a hundred years before they were born, tell me it was not so in his day; that heaven lay about him in his infancy; but that none of the article exists either in that loose condition or otherwise for the immature human animal who breaks out of darkness and mystery into this day of gum-rings. If the tremendous pace at which the modern world is going knocks me up at forty, and compels me to keep my stall for a year ot valetudinarianism, I am asked to remember what a hale old fellow the same inevitable ancestor was at ninety; I am inundated with his exuberance of spirits, overwhelmed with the statistics of his teeth; and invited in the mind's eye (in my own, too, if I know myself!) to take six-mile walks with him before breakfast unassisted by a cane. It is not a pleasant state of mind to be disgusted with one's forefathers, who would, probably, have been very jolly fellows to know, and not the least in the world like the people who are all the time boring us about them. If there is truth in spiritualism, a delegation from those fine old boys will, some of these days, take advantage of a sitting, and rap out an indignant disclaimer of the bosh that is talked in their name. If my grandfather was not a much more unpleasant person than myself, he would scorn to be made a boguey of for the annoyance of his own flesh and blood. Any man of well-regulated mind must prefer utter oblivion among his descendants to such perpetuation as that of Mr. Wilfer.

"Your grandpapa," retorted Mrs. Wilfer, with an awful look, and in an awful tone, "was what I describe him to have been, and would have struck any of his grandchildren to the earth who presumed to question it."

If our ancestors could return to the earth, it is little likely that their first inclination would be to goody themselves over the excellence of their own period, or pull faces at the degeneracy of ours. Sleepers in ill-ventilated, or rather entirely non-ventilated apartments, eaters of inordinate late suppers, five-bottle men, and for the most part wearers of sadly unphilosophical raiment, those sturdy old fox-hunters would acknowledge it just cause for astonishment that their children have any constitutions at all. Little motive for self-laudation would they find in the fact, that, after drawing out their account with Nature to the last dime, they had taken a respectable first-cabin passage to the Infinite Boulogne just before the great Teller said "No funds," and shoved back their checks through the window, leaving to their children the heritage of a spotless name and the declaration of physiological bankruptcy.

Nor would they content themselves, I fancy, with the negative ground of mere humility. They would have something very decided to say to the wiseacres, who taunt our wives in the agony of tic-doloureux with the statement that their grandmothers knew nothing of neuralgia. "No!" these generous ancients would retort, "that is the residuary legacy of a generation to whom we left a nervous system of worn-out fiddle strings." To such as talk of that woful novelty diphtheria as a crime of the present age, they would point out the impossibility of a race's throat descending to it without tenderness, a race's blood flowing to it without taint, from ancestors who swaddled their necks in fathoms of cravat, and despised the question of sewage. When I had the gout, and could not stand up for myself, those brave *vieilles moustaches* would stand up for me. "Many a fine old bin of our port," would they exclaim, "has been emptied down through the æons into those innocent toes of thine. I mind me how I smacked my lips over that very bottle whose broken glass now grinds around, red-hot, in the articulation of thy metatarsal phalanges. Dancing at thy fair great-grandmother's wedding, I slaked the thirst of many vigorous sarabands in that identical ruby nectar, which, turned by the alchemy of generations into acid blood, now through thy great toe distils in gouts of fiery torture. I danced; — thou, poor Serò-natus, dancest not, but dost pay the piper."

Suppose that our returning ancestors regarded us in the intellectual and spiritual, as well as the physical aspect, they must find still less reason to put on airs of superiority. If, in the sphere where they have been lately moving, improvement goes on as fast as we believe, they may be expected to wonder that the theological and scholastic training of their own earthly day has not resulted in a present race of imbeciles and fetish-worshippers, or Torquemadas and madmen. With thankful astonishment will they revere that nature whose boundless elasticity and self-repair has brought bright and self-reliant, even though sometimes a trifle too pert and iconoclastic, Young America from loins burdened, through all their period of cartilage, with five days and a half per week of grammar-grinding, a Saturday afternoon of "keeping in for marks," and a seventh day which should have been the Lord's, but was conspicuously liker the devil's.

Woman, religion, and the forefathers are all the victims of a false quality of reverence. The world has immemorially paid them in the coin of lip-service for the privilege of using their sacredness as a yoke. They are defrauded of their true power by the hands that waft them hypocritical incense; bought off the ground where their influence might be precious and permanent, by the compliment of a moment, or the ceremony of a day. We pick up the fan of the first, and shoulder her out of her partnership in our serious business of living. We build temples for the second, that she may not gad about among our shops, or trouble the doors of our houses. In the third, we do superstitious homage to a mere accident of time, and feel free to neglect the genial lesson of humanity which is eternal.

It is impossible not to reverence our forefathers — those grand old fellows who, long before we rose, got up to build the fires, and shovel the sidewalks of this world. The amount of work which they did was immense; great was their poking and their pushing; their thrashing of arms, and their blowing of fingers. If they sometimes made a compromise with their job; if here and there they left the gutters uncleared, or a heavy drift to thaw over under the sun of modern conscience, and flood our streets with revolution; if they built some of their fires with wet wood, which unto this day smokes the parlors, or even the inmost bed-chambers of mankind, — let us remember how frosty the dawn was, how poorly made were the tools and mittens of the period. All honor to their work, and the will with which they went at it! But when we are asked to regret the rising of the sun; to despise a time of day when there are no more fires to build, no more walks to shovel; or, if such anywhere remain, when there are snow-ploughs and patent-kindling to use in their behoof — distinctly No! — a No as everlasting as Mr. Carlyle's, and spelt with as big a capital.

The mistake of that great writer and minor disciple of the Belated-Owl school to which he belongs, naturally arises, not from the over-development of reverence, to which it is generally ascribed, but from a constitutional divorce between the poetic imagination and the power of analysis. The former faculty, by itself, results in impatience with the meaner actualities of life, — a divine impatience in great poets, a petulant in small ones. Lacking the latter faculty, such persons are in the condition of a near-sighted man placed without chart or compass at the helm of a free-going clipper. Making no allowance for the fact that the blemished and the trivial disappear with distance, and, ignorant of the direction in which humanity must steer, they put out with disgust from a shore where every old clam-shell and rotten wreck is as conspicuous to those, at least, who look for it as the orange-groved cliffs, and the fair retiring stretches of greensward, to voyage for some scarce descried Atlantis gemming the horizon ring with an empurpled roundness born of vapor, time, and space. To such, the future might be a noble course to lay; but that lies beyond the horizon, and impatience is not consistent with faith. On, then, on to the farthest visible,—but westward, while the grand fleet of humanity sails last. Into shadow which drowns the petty details of existence,—not toward a shore which shall be reached only by long buffeting and weary watching, whose noble scenery, glorious with all the temples and trophies of the latest age, shall bear unshamed the scrutiny of the full-risen sun.

The application of scientific processes to the study of history has revealed the steady amelioration of the race. The mail of chivalric giants is brought out of romance's armory to the profane test of a vulgar trying on, and, behold, it is too small for the foot-soldier of to-day. Population everywhere increases, while the rates of mortality diminish. The average longevity of the people of London is greater, by something like twenty-five per cent., than it was a century ago. The improvement of machinery is more and more lifting the yoke of physical labor from the neck of man, leaving his mind freer to cope with the higher problems of his own nature and the universe without. Not as a matter of platform enthusiasm and optimist poetry, but of office statistics, do we know that the world is an easier and better place to live in, and that a man is luckier to be born into it, than in the day of the fathers. So much has changed, and changed for the better. That analysis, which the Carlylists lack, reveals still other changes worked by the course of time in the phenomena of the race,— such changes as concern the habits of society, the styles of literature, the systems of political economy and commercial order, the tenets of philosophy, the schools of art, the forms of government and religion. This analysis further reveals that, while all these functions of life are in their nature endlessly mutable, the organic man, from whom, under all variations, they get their *vis viva*, remains from age to age eternally the same. While each successive generation has its fresh, particular business on the earth,—something to do for the race, which succeeding generations will not have the time, even as prior generations had not the light, to do,—something which is wanted right away,—something for which it was sent and for which the whole machine-shop of time had been shaping the material to be worked by its special hand,—analysis discloses that the capital upon which every business is to be carried on undergoes neither increase nor diminution. There is just as much faith, just as much courage, just as much power in the world as there ever was. They do not show themselves in Runnymedes, because Runnymede has been attended to; nor in wondrous Abbot Sampsons, because monkery is mainly cured. They are not manifest in martyred Edwardses, because at this day Edwards could call a policeman; nor in burning Cranmers, because society has made a phenomenal change in her method with martyrs and shuts them in a refrigerator, where once she chained them to a stake. They do not appear in French Revolutions, because the world has grown through a second American Revolution, grander than the first, and a great representative native has plucked Liberty out of the fire without one scorch of license on her garments. They seek no outlet in crusade, for Jerusalem has been made of as little consequence as Barnegat, by the fulfilment of the promise, —

"The hour cometh when ye shall neither in this mountain, nor yet in Jerusalem, worship the Father, . . . when the true worshippers shall worship him in spirit and in truth."

I have a little butcher, who is Cœur de Lion in the small. He does not split heads nor get imprisoned in castles, but has the same capricious force, the same capacity for affront-taking, the same terribleness of retribution, and the same power of large, frank forgiveness which belonged to the man who broke the skulls of the Saracens and pardoned his own assassin. I went to school to Frederick the Great. He did not take snuff nor swear in high Dutch, and it was his destiny to be at the head, not of an army of men, but of one hundred as unmanageable boys as ever played hawkey or "fought pillows" in the dormitory. His solution of difficulties was as prompt, his decisions were as inexorable, he had as irascible a temper and as admirable a faculty of organization as his Prussian prototype's. Calvin and

Servetus discuss their differences at my dinner-table; the former possesses all his old faith in the inscrutable; the latter all his ancient tendency to bring everything alleged to the tribunal of science, and I may add that Calvin has as little doubt as ever of the propriety of having Servetus cooked, — only he postpones the operation, and expects to see it done without his help. I am acquainted with Sir Philip Sidney, the courtly knight and the melodious poet. The chivalry with which he jousted at Kenilworth and fought at Zutphen are hourly needed in the temptations and harassments of a broker's office, and many's the hard day through which it has borne him with honor. The pen which he devotes to the Muses is as facile as in the Arcadian time, — though the sturdy lance he used to set in rest is substituted by another pen, of the fat office type, consecrated to the back of gold certificates and the support of an unmediævally expensive family.

Looking in all directions round the world, I find the old nobleness, — the primeval sublimities of love and courage, faith and justice, which have always kept humanity moving, and will keep it to the end. In no age has the quantity of this nobleness been excessive, but so much of it as exists is an imperishable quantity. It is a good interred with no man's bones; it is the indispensable preventive of the world's annihilation. Carlyle has been praised for the epigrammatic assertion that nothing can be kept without either life or salt. This is true, but not the whole truth; salt will keep beeves, but as for nations and races which have lost their savor, wherewithal shall they be salted? The fact that mankind survive at all is the proof that ages have not tainted them with putrescence. Things live only by the good that there is in them, and the interests to which they appeal; the fields which open to man, in our own day, are so much vaster and massier than they were in the day of our fathers, that the tax on the activities of the race could not be met by our capital of life if we had lost one particle of the good which supported them.

When I look at the fathers, I recollect that courage and love, faith and justice, have no swallowing horizon, while all that is petty and base succumbs in one generation to the laws of perspective. It is pleasanter thus. At the grave of the old schoolmaster who flogged us, we remember the silver hair and the apple he gave us once, — never the rattan. "We had fathers after the flesh who corrected us, and we gave them reverence," nothing but reverence, when we leaned with tearful eyes over their vacant chairs. If I have ever quarrelled with my friend, when he can return to me no more, I make up with his memory by canonizing him. The tendency to do thus is among the loveliest and divinest things in our nature. But it is a still lovelier and diviner thing to anticipate the parallax of time and look upon the present with the same loving, teachable, and reverent eyes, which shall be bent upon it from the standpoint of coming generations. He to whom the beauty and nobleness of his own time are, throughout all that he deplores in it and in himself, the conspicuous objects of love and veneration, — who extends the allowance of the dead to the faults of the living, — from whom no personal disappointments can ever take away his faith in the abiding divinity of his kind, — need never fear that his judgment of the fathers will be a churlish and disrespectful one. The only object which such a man can have in recalling the vices and defects of older generations is to establish their kinship with his own, to prove his era's legitimacy against philosophers who find only pettiness in the present and grandeur in the past. If he cannot make them see the good side by which the modern family receives blood from the ancient, there shall not be any bend sinister on his escutcheon because he neglects to show them the bad one, though he would rather vindicate his lineage the other way. To him the organic unity of mankind, throughout all generations, is dearer than the individual reputation of any one of them.

Having the faith of this organic unity he can look at the errors of the forefathers without pain. They lessen neither his love nor his respect for them. Who is there that would care to know king David only as a very respectable Jew, in a Sunday-school book, who was always successful, invariably pious, and passed his time wholly in playing hymns on a harp with a golden crown upon his head? To almost all young readers, and many an old one, the vindictive psalms seem a shocking inexplicability in the sacred canon. The philosopher, however, feels with the illiterate preacher, "It is a comfort to us poor erring mortals, my brethren, to remember that on one occasion even, David, beloved of the Lord, said not only, 'I am mad,' but 'I am fearfully and wonderfully mad?'" Not that it would be any comfort to us if that were all we possess of him; but we also have the record of his getting over it. I once knew a little boy who learned to swear out of the psalms, and it must be acknowledged that of good round curses there is in no tongue a much fuller armory. Conscientious persons, who want to damn their enemies without committing sin, no doubt often sit down and read an execratory psalm with considerable relief to their minds. Not in this spirit do men skilled in human nature peruse the grand rages of the many-sided fighting bard; not because they would cloak their errors with the kingly shadow of his own, do they rejoice that he exists for us to-day just where the rude, large simplicity of his original Hebrew left him, and that tame-handed biography has never been able to pumice him down into a demi-god. They are glad because these things prove him human and imitable. If his stormy soul triumphed over itself; if he could be beloved of the Infinite at a moment when the surges of both outer and inner vicissitude seemed conspiring to sweep him away, then we cease to hear his swearing or the clamor of his despair; and to us, whose modern spirits are not exempt from flood and hurricane, his grand voice chants only cheer down the centuries, and we know that there is love caring and victory waiting for us also in our struggle, since we are not the lonely anomalies of time.

As with David so with all the men of the past,—it gives us no pain to find that they were not a whit nearer perfection than ourselves. We do not regret their superseded customs, nor wish them restored in the living age. He who takes them from the time of which they are a congruous part and seeks to import them into a day which has no explanatory relevance to them, so far from showing them reverence, is like a man who, to compel the recognition of his grandfather's tombstone, strips it of its moss, scrubs it with soap and sand, and sets it up on Broadway among signs and show-cases. Their opinions are not final with us, because every age brings new proofs, and every generation is a new court of appeal. Their business methods are framed upon a hypothesis which does not include the telegraph or the steam-engine. Where a man can persuade his correspondents to send their letters by the coach and their goods by the freight-wagon, he may adjust himself very comfortably to the good old way by which his grandfather made a fortune and preserved his health to a great age. Until he gets his mail weekly and answers it all in a batch, recuperating from that labor by the sale of merchandise, one box to an invoice, he is simply absurd to lament over the rapidity with which fortunes are made at this day, and eulogize the "sure and slow" process by which a lifetime whose sole principle was the avoiding of risks attained the same object. As if the whole problem of life were not how to secure, as quick as possible, all the material good necessary for living, in order to leave the kind free for all its higher functions of self-development and discipline. As if money were not a mere expression of the extent to which a man has subordinated the forces of the world to his own use, — a thing, therefore, which naturally comes quicker to a generation which has taken all the great atmospheric and imponderable couriers into its service!

The true use of ancestors is not slavish; we do not want them for authority, but for solace. If my grandfather could come back, he certainly would be too much of a gentleman to sit down on my hat or put his feet on my piano; and how much less would he crush my convictions or trample on my opinions! He would be equally too much of a business-man to interfere in the responsibilities of any practical course I might take, when he had not looked into the books of the concern, taken account of its stock, or consulted the world's market-list for an entire generation. He would do what any man would be proud to have his grandfather do, — take the easiest and most distinguished chair at the fireside, and tell us night by night, the story of his life. What roars of laughter would applaud his recollection of jokes uttered by some playmate of his boyhood. They would seem so droll to us at the distance of a hundred years, though a contemporary might have uttered them without raising a smile on our faces. What mingling of tears and laughter would there be when he related some simple little family drama,—its pathos depending on incidents as slender as the death of Auld Robin Gray's cows, but like the wonderful song, in which those animals have part interest, going unerringly to the fountains of the human heart! How would we double up our fists, how red would we grow in the face when he told us, in the most unadorned, dispassionate way, about the cruel creditor who foreclosed a mortgage on him and turned him and our grandmother into the street, just after the birth of their first child, our father; and when he came to the passage where the kind friend steps in and says, "here are five hundred dollars,—pay me when you are able," how many girls there would be sobbing, and men violently blowing their noses! If we had belonged to the period of the foreclosure and been next-door neighbors to the mortgagor, the thing might have impressed us simply as the spectacle of a young couple with a baby who couldn't meet their quarterly payments, and were obliged to curtail their style of living. The thing still happens, and that is the way we look at it. But when grandpapa relates it, nothing in the domestic line we ever saw upon the stage seems half so touching. The littlest school-boy feels a roseate fascination hovering around the dogs that went after squirrels with that venerable man when he wore the roundabout of his far-off period; there is glamour about the mere fact that then, as now, there were dogs, and there were squirrels; and as the grandchild hears of the boughs which hung so full, the crisp leaves which crackled so frostily those many, many falls ago — a strange delight comes over him, and he seems to be going out chestnutting in the morning of the world.

What we want of one, we want of all the grandfathers of the race, — their story. Their value is that they take the experience of human life, and hold it a sufficient distance from us to be judged in its true proportions, That experience in all ages is a solemn and a beautiful, a perilous, yet a glorious thing. We are too near the picture to appreciate it, as it appears in our own day, though all its grand motives are the same. We rub our noses against the nobilities and cannot see them. The foreground weed is more conspicuous than the background mountain. When the grandfathers carry it from us, and hang it on the wall of that calm gallery where no confusing cross-lights of selfish interest any longer interfere, the shadows fall into their proper places, the symbolisms of the piece are manifest, and above all minor hillocks, above all clouds of storm, unconscious of its earthquake struggles and its glacier scars, Human Nature stands an eternal unity, its peak in a clear heaven full of stars. We recognize that unity and all things become possible to us, for thereby even the commonest living is glorified.

AT EVE.

AT EVE.

"IT is almost time for John to come home, I guess," and the young wife rose from her sewing and put the tea-kettle over the bright fire on the clean-swept hearth. Then she pulled the table out into the middle of the floor, right to the spot where she knew the setting sun would soon shine through the latticed window; for John loved to see the light play upon the homely cups and saucers, and pewter spoons; he said it reminded him of the fairy stories, where they ate off gold dishes. She went about her work swiftly, but very quietly. Once there had been a time when the little cottage rang early and late with the sound of her glad voice. But then a pair of little feet crept over the floor, and a tiny figure had raised itself up by the very table whose cloth was now so smooth and unruffled by the small awkward hands.

When Margery had put the golden butter, the jug of cream, and the slice of sweet honey on the table, she went to the door to look for John. A narrow path, skirted on one side by waving corn-fields, on the other by pastures and orchards, stretched from the cottage down to the broader road that led to the village. The sun was already low in the sky, and threw across the path the shadow of the old apple-tree that stood beside the house. Margery remembered how full of pink and white blossoms the tree had been that spring when she first came here as John's bride, and how they showered down like snow, while now a ripe apple occasionally dropped from the branches with a heavy plump.

"Here comes John at last," she said in a low voice, as she saw him approaching from the village. He was yet a considerable distance off, but Margery's bright eyes discerned that he was not alone. Beside him walked a girl, whom Margery had known already while they were both children. Mary was called handsome by the village lads; but she was poor, and she and her father helped to do field work, on the neighboring farms, in the busiest seasons of the year.

As she and John advanced, Margery noticed that they seemed engaged in earnest conversation. Then John stood still and gave her his hand. The girl seized it eagerly and put it to her lips, and looking up at him once, turned around and walked back to the village, while John hastened on with longer steps.

Margery's lips quivered. She did not wait for John at the door, but turned back into the house, and was busied at the hearth when he came in.

"Well, wify, how goes it this evening?" he asked in his cheery voice, which always reminded Margery of the time when he used to add, "And how is my little pet darlint?" and pick the baby up from the floor. The tones of his voice had grown almost kinder and more cheerful since, if that were possible, though he always gazed around the room with a vague kind of look, as if he half-expected to see the baby toddle up to him from some corner.

"Thank you, John, all goes as well as usual. You are late to-night."

"Yes, there was something to detain me," he said, as he took down the tin-basin and filled it with water, to wash his sunburnt face and hands. A shadow flitted over Margery's face, but it was gone again when they sat down to table. It was still light enough to see without a candle, though the golden sunbeams John loved so much had faded long ago. He talked cheerily of the crops, and of harvest-time, and of the excellent prospects for the coming winter. There was no occasion for Margery to say much, and she was glad of it.

Then she quickly cleared the table, and John sat down by the hearth, lighted his pipe, and laid his evening paper across his knee to be read afterwards by candle-light. While Margery washed the dishes there was no sound in the room but the clatter of the cups and spoons, and the monotonous ticking of the old-fashioned clock in the corner. Margery sometimes glanced over at John, who sat smoking and looking into the fire. At last he got up, lit the candle, and, going up to Margery, he asked, "What's the matter, Margery? You are uncommonly silent to-night."

She stopped in her work, and hung the towel over her arm.

"John," she said, looking straight at him, with a strange light in her brown eyes, and her face rather pale, "I want to go home."

An expression half of pain, half of astonishment, came into John's honest face. He too was a shade paler, and the candle trembled a little in his hand as he asked, —

"Is the house too lonely again, Margery? You did say you wanted to go home for a spell, after, after — but I thought you had got contented again."

She had turned away from him as she answered, —

"Yes, John, the house is lonely again. I see the little hands on all the chairs, and hear the little feet crawling over the floor;" but there was something of coldness in her tone, very unlike the pleading voice in which she had once before made the same request.

"Well, Margery," he went on, after a pause, going to the table and putting the candle upon it, "if you think it will ease your heart to go and see the old folks a little while, I am willing you should."

He never spoke of the utter loneliness that fell upon him at the thought of her going away, and how to him, too, the dim room was full of the golden hair and the blue eyes of his child.

She said nothing.

"When will you come back, Margery?" he asked, after another pause.

"I don't know, John."

"When do you think of going?"

"On Monday morning, if you can spare the horse to take me over."

"I think I can, Margery; but I shall be sorry to lose my little wify so soon," he could not help saying, as he laid his rough hand on her hair, with so soft a touch that the tears started to her eyes.

"I shall ask Mary to come here and keep house for you, while I am away," she said. "Mary is used to our ways, and can do for you very well."

"Mary?" asked John, "I reckon she will be busy enough at harvest-time. I need nobody when you are gone. I can live single again," with a half smile; "but just as you think, Margery."

Nothing more was said on the subject. Margery took up her sewing, and John his paper. But he did not read very attentively that evening, but often stopped and looked long and intently at Margery, who kept her eyes steadily on the busy needle that was flying to and fro in her fingers. It was a Saturday, and John tired with a week's hard labor. So the fire was raked for the night, the old clock wound up, and the little kitchen soon dark and silent.

Next morning Margery awoke bright and early. So early indeed, that through the open window of the bedroom she could see the pink clouds floating in the sky, and felt the cool wind that always goes before the rising of the sun. The swallows under the roof were just waking up, and beginning to twitter half-dreamily. With her hands folded under her head, Margery lay musing for a long while. Somehow her whole life passed before her on this still, holy Sunday morning. She remembered when she used to play barefoot in the little brook or sit on warm summer afternoons on the straight-rowed wooden benches of the village school. How the years had sped by like a single day, and she was a grown young girl. Then John came and courted her, and then —. The sun had come up, and played in bright lights over the ceiling, while on the floor quivered the shadows of the rose-leaves from outside before the window. The church-bell in the village began to ring. Margery listened to the sounds, as they came borne on the soft breeze, across the waving corn-fields. She looked out at the blue sky and thought of heaven, and the blessed angels singing and rejoicing there. She thought of her child, and of John, and of herself. A mingled feeling of joy and pain, of calm and unrest, crept into her heart. She felt the tears rising to her eyes again, but she would not let them. She sprang up, dressed hastily, and went softly down-stairs, while John slept heavily on.

As Margery entered the kitchen, the cat got up from her rug, stretched her legs and yawned, and then came forward to be petted. On the next Sunday, Mary would probably be here to give pussy her milk, and stroke her soft, glossy back. Margery threw open the door to let in the beautiful fresh morning air. The dew lay sparkling on the grass and flowers. Down there on the road was the spot where John and Mary had parted last night. Margery turned away and shut the door again. Then she bestirred herself to get breakfast.

When John came down to it, Margery thought his step sounded heavier than she had ever heard it before.

"Will you go to church this morning, Margery?" he asked, when the simple meal was over.

"No, John, I guess not."

"Well, Margery, I am going. I will come home as soon as service is over; but I think it will do me good."

"John, will you promise me to" ——

"What, Margery?"

"This afternoon, after I have got ready to go, will you come once more with me to the — the grave?"

"Yes, Margery, yes."

She helped him on with his best coat, brought him the prayer-book, and then watched him from the window as he walked down the road with slow steps.

Margery wondered what could be the matter with herself that morning. She felt so tired that her feet almost refused to carry her. A hundred times in her simple household duties, she paused to take breath, and sat down to rest so often, that John came home from church and to dinner, almost before it was ready. He praised the cookery; but the dishes were taken almost untouched off the table again, and when everything was cleared away, Margery said, —

"I must go upstairs now, John, to get ready. I want to take some of my clothes with me."

He sat on the doorstep, holding his pipe, which had

gone out, between his fingers, and only nodded his head, and said nothing. Margery went up to the bedroom, and began to open closets and drawers, and pack articles of clothing into a small trunk. At last she unlocked the great old bureau, and took out a pile of tiny dresses and aprons, a tin cup, and a few bright marbles, and stowed them carefully away in the trunk. A pair of small, worn-out leather shoes, turned up at the toes, stood in the drawer yet. Should she carry both these away, too? No, she thought, as she brushed away the tears that had fallen upon it, one she had better leave John. She put it resolutely back, locked the drawer, and laid the key on the top of the bureau. Now there was nothing more to be done. She looked around the room. Yes, that was to be readied up a little, so that John might not miss her too much for the first day or two. So she polished the chairs and the bureau, and carefully dusted the mantle-piece, with the red and white china dog and the kneeling china angel that stood there. Then she herself was to be dressed; she had almost forgotten that altogether. She opened her trunk once more, and took out the dress John loved best to see her in.

Several hours had slipped by while she was thus employed, and now the village-clock struck five. She hastened down. John still sat on the doorstep where she had left him.

"John, dear, I did not think it was so late. It is time to go to the graveyard. Are you ready to come?"

He looked up as if he had been dreaming, but rose and said, "Yes, Margery."

He shut the house-door, and they turned into a path to the rear of the cottage. For some distance this road, too, was skirted on both sides by fields of ripened corn. John passed his hand thoughtlessly over the heavy ears, and now and then pulled one up, and swung it round in the air. Neither of them spoke, and for a long while there was no other sound but the rustle of their steps.

The path at length turned aside and led to a high plateau that overlooked the valley, in which deep shadows were already beginning to fall. Blue mists crept over the foot of the mountains, while their tops were yet lit up by the sun. The smoke from the chimneys rose up into the air, and the shouts of the village children, playing on the meadow, faintly came up from below. There under that great oak, the only tree for some distance around, John had first asked Margery to be his wife. Involuntarily the steps of both faltered as they drew near the spot, but neither stopped. Margery glanced up at John; she could not see his face, for his head was turned, and he seemed to be attentively looking at something down in the valley.

Another turn in the road, and the small cemetery, with the white stones that gleamed between the dark cypress-trees, rose up before them. In silence they found their way to the little grave. John seated himself, without a word, on a mound opposite, Margery knelt down and pulled some dried leaves off the rose-tree she had planted, and bound the ivy further up on the white marble cross. She felt that John watched her, but did not look up at him. Though she tried hard to keep them back, the tears would fill her eyes again and again, so that she could hardly see to pluck up the few weeds that had grown among the grass. When that was completed, she covered her face with her hands and tried to pray. She wanted to ask that John might be happy while she was away, and that, — but her head swam round, and she found no words. She raised her eyes, and glanced at John through her fingers. He sat with his back toward her now, but she saw that his great, strong frame trembled with half-suppressed sobs.

"O John!" she cried, bursting into tears. She only noticed yet that he suddenly turned around, and then closed her eyes, as he clasped her in his arms. For a time she heard nothing but the sound of her own low weeping, and the throbbing of John's heart. Suddenly she looked up, and said, —

"O John, dear, dear John, please, please forgive me!"

"Margery," he answered, in as firm a tone as he could command, "don't talk so."

"Oh, but, John, I did not want to go away only because the house was so lonely, but because, — because," —

"Because what, Margery?" he asked, astonished.

"O John, because I — I thought you loved Mary better than me, because I saw you together so many times in the last weeks; and she kissed your hand last night."

John's clasp about Margery relaxed, and his arms sank down by his side. His tears were dried now, and his earnest blue eyes fixed upon Margery with a dumb, half-unconscious expression of surprise and pain. She could not bear the look, and covered her face with her hands again.

"No, Margery," he said, slowly, "I only saw Mary because," —

Margery raised her head.

"John, dear John, don't talk about it! I don't believe it any more! I know I was a bad, foolish wife! Only love me again, and forgive me, dear, dear John! Oh, I don't believe it any more!" and she took his right hand and kissed it, as Mary had done.

"Wont you forgive me, John? I will never, never go away from you," she pleaded, while the tears streamed down her face.

He took her in his arms once more, and kissed her lips.

The red evening sunlight had crept away from the little grave, and the dusk was fast gathering about it. Margery bent down and kissed the white marble cross; then they turned their steps homeward, Margery holding John's hand like a child.

"I must unpack my clothes again to-night," she said, after a while. "I have all the baby's little things in my trunk, but, John, I was going to leave you one of the little shoes."

She felt her hand clasped closer in his.

"Margery," he said then, "I think I had better tell you about Mary."

"John, dear John, didn't I tell you I don't believe that any more," she answered, with another pleading look.

"No Margery, it is not that, but I guess you might help us. You never knew that Mary's father is getting very bad in the way of drinking. Since his house was burnt down, and he lost his property, he has been going on in that way. Mary takes it dreadful hard, and wont let the news get about, if she can help it. She thinks so much of you, and she says you used to like her father so well, that she wouldn't have you know for almost any money. So I promised not to tell you. She has come to me many and many a time, crying, and begging me to help her. She works as hard as she can, but her father takes all she gets ; so they are very poor. When you saw us yesterday, I had given her money to pay their rent. She wants to raise money enough to take him to the Asylum, because there he may be cured. I promised her to get him some decent clothes."

"O John, I will sew them. Poor Mary ! and you needn't tell her who sewed them."

"That's right, Margery ! "

They had reached the house by this time, and John opened the door. The kettle was singing over the hearth, and the bright tin pans against the wall shone in the firelight. On the doorstep Margery turned around, and, throwing her arms around John's neck, said softly, —

"John, I am glad I am going to stay."

When they had entered, John lit the candle, and while Margery was getting supper, took up yesterday's unfinished paper. He read very attentively this evening, but suddenly stopped, and Margery saw the paper tremble in his hand. Then he rose, gave it to her, and said, in a husky voice, —

"Read that, Margery."

Margery read. Then the paper dropped, and with a fresh burst of tears she once more threw her arms about John's neck.

In one corner of the paper that lay neglected on the floor was the poem: —

"As through the land at eve we went,
And plucked the ripened ears,
We fell out, my wife and I,
Oh, we fell out, I know not why,
And kissed again with tears.

"For when we came where lies the child
We lost in other years;
There above the little grave,
Oh, there above the little grave,
We kissed again with tears."

BROKEN IDOLS.

BROKEN IDOLS.

OT long since, it was my misfortune to be inveigled into attending one of the semi-periodical "Exhibitions" of the —— Institute, a seminary for young ladies. I say it was my misfortune, because, to please my better half, I abandoned the joys of my fireside, my book, and my slippers, to stand for two hours by an open window, with a cold draft blowing on my back; hearing, now and then, a few words of the sentimental and "goody" platitudes of which the young ladies' essays were composed, — the reading of which was interspersed with pyrotechnic performances on the piano-forte, which the programme was kind enough to inform me were "The Soldiers' Chorus from Faust," "Duette from Norma," etc. I was fortunate in having a programme to enlighten me.

There was nothing remarkable about the "Exhibition," except that, in the dozen essays which were read, all the verses of Longfellow's "Psalm of Life" were quoted, and that through them all there ran a dismal monotone of morbid sentiment. One young lady, who had a beautiful healthy bloom on her cheeks and wore quite a quantity of comfortable and elegant clothing, uttered a very touching wail over her buried hopes, her vanished joys, and the mockery of this hollow-hearted world. She stated that all that's brightest must fade, — that "this world is all a fleeting show, for man's illusion given," — that "our hearts, though stout and brave, still, like muffled drums, are beating funeral marches to the grave;" and much more of the same sort. She was impressed with the fact that Time is an iconoclast, — which last word seemed to strike her as one of the finest in the dictionary.

This is very true. Time does smash our idols continually; but should we lament and sing dirges and make ourselves generally uncomfortable on that account? Because the geese that we thought swans have turned out to be only geese after all, should we go into mourning for our "buried hopes," and "vanished joys"? That we outgrow our youthful fancies is no more a cause for sentimental regret than that we outgrow our youthful jackets. For myself, I can look upon the ashes of my early loves, — and their name was legion, — with as few tears as I bestow upon the ragged remnants of my early trousers.

A number of years ago my young heart's fresh affections were lavished upon the bright-eyed girl whose father kept a little candy-shop and bakery across the way, and who with her own fair hands often gave me striped sticks of stomach-ache for my pennies, and sometimes, when I was penniless, sweetened my lot with a few peppermint drops, telling me to pay for them when I came into my fortune. Many a time have I stood by the lighted window of the little shop, heedless of the bell that summoned me to my nightly bread and milk, watching her trip about among the jars of candy and barrels of nuts, tying up parcels and making change with a grace that seemed unsurpassable. But there was a red-haired, scorbutic youth who drove the baker's bread-cart, and also drove me to distraction. He was always flinging my youth into my face and asking if my mother was aware of my whereabouts. At last a grave suspicion forced itself upon my mind that Lizzie looked upon him with favor and made light of my juvenile demonstrations. Time proved that my suspicion was well founded; for one day a carriage stopped in front of the little shop, out of which sprang the scorbutic young man, clad in unusually fine raiment, including a gorgeous yellow vest and immaculate white gloves. He was followed by a solemn-looking person, who wore a very black coat and a very white choker. They passed through the shop and went up the back stairs. After a while they returned, and with them Lizzie, all smiles and blushes and ribbons and a bewitching pink bonnet. The carriage was driven away and my idol was smashed.

Straightway I builded me another, which was in turn broken, and followed by another and another. Sometimes it was the dashing highwayman, whose life and brilliant exploits I furtively made myself acquainted with, out in the wood-house, and whose picture, in profuse curls, enormous jack-boots, and immense expanse of coat-flap, graced the yellow covers of the Claude Duval series of novels. Anon it was the great Napoleon seated so proudly, — in cheap lithograph, — upon the extreme hind-quarters of his fiery charger, and pointing with aspiring hand toward the snowy Alps, that I set up and worshipped.

Nor was I free from relapses of the tender passion. About the time that my first love, Lizzie, was putting the third of her red-haired progeny into pantaloons, and torturing his fiery elf-locks into an unsightly "roach," and when I was a freshman in college, I became convinced that the light of my life shone from a certain window in Miss Peesley's boarding-school; for behind that window a comely maiden, with golden hair and eyes of heavenly blue, slept and studied and ate sweetmeats and read Moore's melodies. My heart was hers entirely, as was also my spare coin, — for we had specie in those days, — which I converted into valentines and assorted candies and "The Language of Flowers," for her especial use and behoof. I worshipped her at church, as she sat, with a bevy of other girls, aloft in the gallery, the entrance to which was guarded by the ancient and incorruptible damsel who taught algebra in Miss Peesley's academy, and who also marshalled the young ladies to and from church, keeping them under her eye, and putting to rout any audacious youth who endeavored to walk with one of them. It was for her that I bought a flute, and with much difficulty so far mastered it as to play "Sweet Home" and "What fairy-like music," — in performing which, standing in the snow under her window at midnight's witching hour, I caught a terrible cold, besides being threatened with arrest by a low-bred policeman for making an unseemly noise in the night-time, — as if I were a calliope. It was to bow to her that I neglected to split and carry in my Saturday's wood, and stood on the street-corner all the afternoon, for which I was soundly rated at night by my venerable father, who also improved the occasion by repeating his regular lecture upon my inattentions to study and general neglect of duty.

So great was my infatuation that I manifested an unheard-of anxiety about the details of my dress. I even went so far as to attend the Friday evening "Receptions" at the academy, where Miss Peesley graciously gave the young gentlemen an opportunity to see and converse with the young ladies, under her own supervision. It was a dismal business, — sitting bolt upright in a straight-backed, hair-cushioned chair, under the gaze of Miss P. and her staff, smiling foolishly at some dreary, pointless sally of Miss Van Tuyl's, who taught rhetoric and was remarkably sprightly for one of her years, — crossing and uncrossing my legs uneasily, and endeavoring to persuade myself that I was "enjoying the evening." Nevertheless, I made desperate attempts to be happy even under these adverse circumstances.

And what was my reward?

There came to college a young man who was reputed to be a poet. He wore his hair long and parted in the middle, was addicted to broad Byronic collars, could take very pretty and pensive attitudes, and was an adept in the art of leaning his head abstractedly upon his hand. He at once became that terrible thing among the ladies, a lion. And he was a very impudent lion. Regardless of my claims and feelings, he sent to her, whom I had fondly called mine own, an acrostic valentine of his own composition, taking care that she should know from whom it came. The result was that I was — as we Western people would term it — "flopped!"

And so another idol was smashed.

Then came a reaction. I scorned the sex and sought balm for my wounded feelings in the worst pages of Byron.

Having by this time attained the sophomoric dignity, I discovered that the end and aim of existence was to be *fast,* — that the divine significance of life consisted in drinking villanous whiskey "on the sly," and proclaiming the fact by eating cardamom seeds; in stealing gates and the clapper of the chapel bell; in devouring half-cooked chickens, purloined from professional coops; in hazing freshmen; in playing euchre for "ten cents a corner;" and in parading the streets at midnight, singing "Landlord, fill the flowing bowl," and vociferously urging some one to "rip and slap and set 'em up ag'in, all on a summer's day." I smoked vile Scarfalatti tobacco in a huge Dutch pipe, wore a blue coat with brass buttons, a shocking hat, and my trousers tucked into my boots, — which after my great disappointment befell me I ceased to black with any degree of regularity, — and regulated my language according to a certain slangy work called "Yale College Scrapes."

I am inclined to look upon these youthful pranks not as unpardonable sins, though I freely admit their utter folly, but as the vagaries of immature *genius*, — if I may say so, — scorning to walk decorously, because other people do, struggling to throw off the fetters of conventionality, burning to distinguish itself in some new and original way, striking out from the beaten paths, — to repent of it afterward. For it does not take many years to teach one that the beaten paths are the safest; and I have often wished that I had had a tithe of the application and assiduity of "Old Sobriety," as we rapid youngsters called the Nestor of the class, who plodded on from morn till dewy eve and far into the night, and quietly carried off the honors from the brilliant geniuses, who wore flash neckties and shone at free-and-easys. But what thoughtless college-boy does not prefer worshipping at the shrine of the fast goddess to treading the straight and safe paths of propriety? It takes time and one or two private interviews with a committee of the Faculty to rid him of his delusion.

I have been making these confessions to show that I, too, as well as the handsome and healthy young lady whose essay furnishes my text, have had some joys that are vanished and some hopes that are buried.

But I do not therefore find that this world is a dark and dreary desert. I do not rail at life as a hollow mockery, nor long to lay my weary head upon the lap of earth. On the contrary, the longer I live in this world, the better I like it. It is a jolly old world, after all; and, though Time is an iconoclast and does smash our idols with a ruthless hand, it is only to purify our vision; and, as the fragments tumble and the dust settles, we see the true, the beautiful, and the joyous in life more clearly. I know that life has its disappointments and crosses; but I think that it is too short for sentimental lamentation over them. In homely phrase, "There is no use in crying over spilt milk." If Dame Fortune frowns, laugh her in the face, and, with a light heart and brave spirit, woo her again, and you will surely win her smile. I am as fully impressed as any one with the fact that this world is not our permanent abiding-place; but that is no reason why we should underrate, abuse, and malign it. There is such a thing as being too other-worldly. The grand truths and beautiful teachings of God's gospel do not conflict with the grandeur, the beauty, and the mystery of God's handiwork, the world; and we can no more afford to despise and dispense with the one than with the other. And it seems to me that we cannot better prepare for enjoying the life hereafter than by a healthy, hearty, rational enjoyment of the one that is here.

Do not, then, O youth, sit down and grow sentimental over your fancied griefs. Do not waste your time in shedding weak tears over the fragments of your broken idols. Kick the rubbish aside, and go on your way, with head erect and heart open to the sweet influences of this bright and beautiful world, and you cannot fail to find it not a "Piljin's Projiss of a Wale," but

> "A sunshiny world, full of laughter and leisure."

In worthy action and healthy enjoyment you will find a cure for all your imaginary woes and all your maudlin fine feelings.

In two little lines lies the clue to an honorable and happy life: —

> "Thou shalt find, by *hearty striving* only
> And *truly loving*, thou canst truly live."

DR. HUGER'S INTENTION.

Dr. Huger's Intention.

DR. HUGER was thirty years old when he deliberately resolved to be in love,—I cannot say "fall in love" of anything so matter-of-fact and well-considered. He made up his mind that marriage was a good thing,—that he was old enough to marry,—finally, that he *would* marry. Then he decided, with equal deliberation, on the qualifications necessary in the lady, and began to look about him to find her. She must be a blonde. Above all things else, he must have her gentle and trustful; and he believed that gentleness and trustfulness inhered in the blue-eyed, fair-haired type of womanhood. She must be appreciative, but not strong-minded,—well-bred, with a certain lady-like perfectness, which could not be criticised, and yet which would always save her from being conspicuous. Not for the world would he have any new-fangled woman's-rights notions about her.

You might fancy it would be a somewhat difficult matter for him to find precisely the realization of this ideal; but here fate befriended him,—fate, who seemed to have taken Dr. Huger under her especial charge, and had been very kind to him all his life. He looked out of his window, after he had come to the resolution heretofore recorded, and saw Amy Minturn tripping across the village green.

Amy was eighteen, — blonde, blue-eyed, innocent, well-bred, unpresuming, without ambition, and without originality. She was very lovely in her own quiet, tea-rose style. Her position was satisfactory; for her father, Judge Minturn, was a man of mark in Windham, and one of Dr. Huger's warmest friends. So, having decided that here was an embodiment of all his "must-haves," the doctor went over that evening to call at the Minturn mansion. Not that the call in itself was an unusual occurrence. He went there often; but hitherto his conversation had been principally directed to the judge, and to-night there was a noticeable change.

Amy was looking her loveliest, in her diaphanous muslin robes, with blue ribbons at her throat, and in her soft light hair. Dr. Huger wondered that he had never before noticed the pearly tints of her complexion, the deep lustrous blue of her eyes, the dainty, flower-like grace of her words and ways. He talked to her, and watched the changing color in her cheeks, and her rippling smiles, until he began to think the falling in love, to which he had so deliberately addressed himself, the easiest and pleasantest thing in the world. She had the prettiest little air of propriety, — half prudish, and half coquettish. She received his attentions with a shy grace that was irresistibly tempting.

He went often to Judge Minturn's after that — not *too* often, for he did not wish to startle his pretty Amy by attentions too sudden or too overpowering; and, indeed, there was nothing in the gentle attraction by which she drew him to hurry him into any insane forgetfulness of his customary moderation. But he liked and approved her more and more. He made up his mind to give her a little longer time in which to become familiar with him, and then to ask her to be his wife.

When he had reached this determination, he was sent for, one August day, to see a new patient, — a certain Miss Colchester. He was thinking about Amy as he went along, — laughing at the foolish old notion concerning the course of true love; for what could run any smoother, he asked himself, than his had? It seemed to him as simple and pretty as an idyl, — the "Miller's Daughter" New Englandized.

> "Oh, that I were beside her now!
>   Oh, will she answer if I call?
> Oh, would she give me vow for vow, —
>   Sweet Amy, — if I told her all?"

he hummed, half unconsciously, as he walked on.

Soon he came in sight of Rock Cottage, the place to which he was going, and began thereupon to speculate about Miss Colchester. Of course she was one of the summer boarders of whom Rock Cottage was full. He wondered whether she were young or old, — whether he should like her, — whether she would be good pay; — and by this time, he had rung the bell, and was inquiring for her of the tidy girl who answered his summons.

He was shown into a little parlor on the first floor, and, pausing a moment at the door, he looked at his patient. A very beautiful woman, he said to himself, but just such an one as he did not like. She sat in a low chair, her back to the window and her face turned toward him. She wore a simple white-cambric wrapper. Her beauty had no external adornment whatever. It shone upon him startlingly and unexpectedly, as if you should open a closet, where you were prepared to find an old family portrait of some stiff Puritan grandmother, and be confronted, instead, by one of Murillo's Spanish women, passionate and splendid. For Miss Colchester was not unlike those Murillo-painted beauties. She had a clear, dark skin, through which the changeful color glowed as if her cheeks were transparent; dark, heavily-falling hair; low brow; great, passionate, slumbrous eyes; proud, straight features. There was nothing like a New-England woman about her. That was Dr. Huger's first thought; and she read it, either through some subtle clairvoyant power, or, a simpler solution, because she knew that every one, who saw her under these cool skies of the temperate zone, would naturally think that thought first. Her full, ripe lips parted in a singular smile, as she said, —

"You are thinking that I am not of the North. You are right. I was born in New Orleans. I am a Creole of the Creoles. I don't like the people here. I sent for you because you were German, at least by descent."

"How did you know it?"

It was an abrupt question for a man of the doctor's habitual grave courtesy; but she seemed to him unique, and it was impossible to maintain his old equipoise in her presence. She had read his thought like a witch. Was there something uncanny about her?

"How did I know you were German?" She smiled. "Because your name suggested the idea, and then I saw you in the street, and your features indorsed the hint your name had given me."

"I am glad that anything should have made you think of me."

It was one of the conventional platitudes, of which self-complacent men, like Dr. Huger, keep a stock on hand for their lady friends. Miss Colchester saw its poverty, and smiled at it, as she answered him,—

"I think of every one with whom I come in contact; and I thought of you, especially, because I intended from the first, if there were a good physician here, to consult him."

The doctor looked into her radiant face.

"Is it possible that you are ill?"

He had sat down beside her by this time, and taken her hand. It gave him a curious sensation as it lay quietly in his. He felt as if there were more life, more magnetism, in it than in any hand he had ever touched.

"That *you* must tell me," she said, quietly. "My heart feels strangely, sometimes; it beats too rapidly, I think, and sometimes very irregularly. I have lived too fast, — suffered and enjoyed too keenly. The poor machine is worn out, perhaps. I look to you to inform me whether I am in danger."

"I must have my stethoscope. I will go for it. Are you sure you can bear the truth?"

She smiled, — a cool smile touched with scorn.

"I have not found life so sweet," she said, "that its loss will trouble me. I only want to know how long I am likely to have in which to do certain things. If you can tell me, I shall be satisfied."

As Dr. Huger went home, he met Amy. Something in the sight of her fresh, blonde beauty, with its fulness of life and health, jarred on his mood. He bowed to her with a preoccupied air, and hurried on. When he went back to Rock Cottage, Miss Colchester was sitting just as he had left her. To sit long at a time in one motionless attitude was a peculiarity of hers. Her manner had always a singular composure, though her nature was impetuous.

He placed over her heart the instrument he had brought, then listened a long time to its beating. He dreaded to tell her the story it revealed to him, and at last made up his mind to evade the responsibility. When he had come to this conclusion, he raised his head.

"I do not feel willing," he said, "to pronounce an opinion. Let me send for a medical man who is older, who has had more experience."

She raised her dark eyes, and looked full in his face.

"You are afraid to tell me, after all I said? Will you not believe that I do not care to live? I shall send for no other physician. I look for the truth from your lips. You find my heart greatly enlarged?"

"I told you I did not like to trust my own judgment; but that *is* my opinion."

"And if you are right I shall be likely to live — how long?"

"Possibly for years. Probably for a few months. There is no help, — I mean, no cure. If you suffer much pain, that can be eased, perhaps."

Miss Colchester was silent a few moments. Dr. Huger could see no change in her face, though he watched her closely. The color neither left her cheeks or deepened in them. He did not see so much as an eyelash quiver. At last she spoke, —

"You have been truly kind, and I thank you. I believe I am glad of your tidings. I think I shall stay here in Windham till the last. I would like one autumn among these grand old woods and hills. I have nothing to call me away. I can do all which I have to do by letter, and my most faithful friend on earth is my quadroon maid who is here with me. She will be my nurse, if I need nursing. And you will be my physician, — will you not?"

"I will when I can help you. At other times, may I not be your friend, and as such come to see you as often as I can?"

"Just as often, — the oftener the better," she answered, with that smile which thrilled him so strangely every time he met it. "I shall always be glad to see you. Your visits will be a real charity; for, except Lisette, I am quite solitary."

He understood by her manner that it was time to go, and took his leave.

That night he walked over to Judge Minturn's. Amy was just as pretty as ever, —just as graceful and gentle and faultless in dress and manner. Why was it that he could not interest himself in her as heretofore? Had the salt lost its savor? His judgment endorsed her as it always had. She was precisely the kind of woman to make a man happy. That pure blonde beauty, with its tints of pearl and pink, was just what he wanted, always had wanted. Why was it that he was haunted all the time by eyes so different from those calm blue orbs of Amy's? He thought it was because his new patient's case had interested him so much in a medical point of view. He was tired, and he made it an excuse for shortening his call.

He went home to sit and smoke and speculate again about Miss Colchester. He seemed to see her wonderful exotic face through the blue smoke-wreaths. Her words and ways came back to him. He had discovered so soon that *she* was no gentle, yielding creature. She had power enough to make her conspicuous anywhere — piquant moods and manners of her own, which a man could find it hard to tame. He was glad, — or thought he was, — that such office had not fallen to his share,

— that the woman he had resolved to marry was so unlike her; yet he could not banish the imperious face which haunted his fancy.

The next day found him again at Rock Cottage; but he waited until afternoon, when all his other visits had been made. It was a warm day; and Miss Colchester was again in white, but in full fleecy robes, whose effect was very different from the simple cambric wrapper she had worn the day before. Ornaments of barbaric gold were in her ears, at her throat, and manacled her wrists. A single scarlet lily drooped low in her hair. She looked full of life, — strong, passionate, magnetic life. Was it possible that he had judged her case aright? Could death come to spoil this wonderful beauty in its prime?

Their talk was not like that of physician and patient. It touched on many themes, and she illuminated each one with the quick brilliancy of her thought. He grew acquainted with her mind in the two hours he spent with her; but her history,— who she was,— whence she came, — why she was at Windham, — remained as mysterious as before. Her maid came in once or twice, and called her "Miss Pauline," and this one item of her first name was all that he knew about her more than he had discovered yesterday. He saw her, — a woman utterly different from the gentle, communicative, impressible, blue-eyed ideal he had always cherished, — a woman with whom, had she been in her full health, his reason would have pronounced it madness to fall in love. How much more would it be madness now, when he knew that she was going straight to her doom,—that when the summer came again, it would shine upon her grave! And yet it seemed as if the very hopelessness of any passion for her made her power over him more fatal.

He went to see her day after day. He did not consciously neglect Amy Minturn, because he did not think about her at all. She was no more to him in those days than last year's roses, which had smelled so sweet to him in their prime. He was absorbed in Pauline Colchester—lived in her life. She accepted his devotion, simply because she did not understand it. If she had been in health, she would have known that this man loved her; but the knowledge of her coming fate must make all that impossible, she thought. So she accepted his friendship with a feeling of entire security; and, though she revealed to him no facts of her material life, admitted him to such close intimacy with her heart and soul as, under other circumstances, he might never have reached in a lifetime of acquaintance.

And the nearer he drew to her the more insanely he loved her,—loved her, though he knew the fate which waited for her, the heart-break he was preparing for himself.

At last he told her. He had meant to keep his secret until she died, but in spite of himself it came to his lips.

In September it was,—one of those glorious autumn days when the year seems at flood-tide, full of a ripe glory, which thrills an imaginative temperament as does no tender verdure of spring, no bravery of summer. Pauline Colchester, sensitive to all such influences as few are, was electrified by it. Dr. Huger had never seen her so radiant, so full of vitality. It seemed to him impossible that she should die. If he had her for his own,—if he could make her happy,—could he not guard her from every shock or excitement, and keep her in such a charmed atmosphere of peace that the worn-out heart might last for many a year?

It was the idlest of lover's dreams, the emptiest and most baseless of hopes, which he would have called any other man insane for cherishing. But he grasped at it eagerly, and, before he knew what he was doing, he had breathed out his longing at the feet of Miss Colchester.

"Is it possible," she said, after a silent space, "that you could have loved me so well? That you would have absorbed into your own the poor remnant of my life, and cherished it to the end? I ought to be sorry for your sake; but how can I, when just such a love is what I have starved for all my life? I have no right to it now. I am Mrs., not Miss, Colchester. I was Pauline Angereau before Ralph Colchester found me and married me. I had money and, I suppose, beauty; perhaps he coveted them both. He made me believe that he loved me with all his heart; and then, when I was once his wife, he began torturing me to death with his neglect and his cruelty. He was a bad man; and I don't believe there is a woman on earth strong enough to have saved him from himself. I bore everything, for two years, in silence. Then I found that it was killing me, and, in one of his frequent absences, I came away to die in peace. When it is all over, Lisette will write to him. He will have the fortune he longed for, without the encumbrance of which he tired so soon. You must not see me any more. Bound as I am, feeling what you feel, there would be sin in our meeting. And yet I shall die easier for knowing that, once in my life, I have been loved for myself alone."

Then Dr. Huger rose to go. To-morrow, perhaps he could combat those scruples of hers; but to-day, there was no more to be said to this woman whom another man owned. To-morrow, he could tell better how nearly he could return to the quiet ways of friendship, — whether it would be possible for him to tend her, brother-like, to the last, as he had meant to do before he loved her. He took her hand a moment, and said, in a tone which he tried so hard to make quiet that it almost sounded cold, —

"I must go now. I dare not stay and talk to you. I will come again to-morrow."

"Yes, to-morrow."

Her face kindled, as she spoke, with a strange light as of prophecy. What "to-morrow" meant to her he did not know. He turned away suddenly, for his heart was sore; and, as he went, he heard her say, speaking very low and tenderly, —

"God bless you, Francis Huger."

The next day he went again to Rock Cottage. He

had fought his battle and conquered. He thought now that he could stay by her to the end, and speak no word, look no look, which should wrong her honor or his own. He asked for her at the door as usual; and they told him she had paid her bill that morning, and left. She had come, they said, no one knew from whence; and no one knew where she had gone. She had left no messages and given no address.

Dr. Huger understood that this was something she had meant to keep secret from him of all others. Was he never to see her again? When she had said, "Yes, to-morrow," could she have meant the long to-morrow, when the night of death should be over? He turned away, making no sign of disappointment,—his sorrow dumb in his heart; and, as he went, her voice seemed again to follow him,—

"God bless you, Francis Huger."

For two months afterward, he went the round of his daily duties in a strange, absent, divided fashion. He neither forgot nor omitted anything; yet he saw as one who saw not, and heard with a hearing which conveyed to his inward sense no impression. *She* was with him everywhere. All the time, he was living over the brief four weeks of their acquaintance, in which, it seemed to him, he had suffered and enjoyed more than in all the rest of his lifetime. Every day, every hour, he expected some message from her. He felt a sort of conviction that she would not die until he had seen her again. He thought, at last, that his summons to her side had come.

11

He opened, one day, a letter directed in a hand with which he was not familiar. He read in it, with hurrying pulses, only these words : —

"Madame Pauline Angereau Colchester is dead. I obey her wish in sending you these tidings.

"LISETTE."

From the letter had dropped, as he unfolded it, a long silky tress of dark hair. He picked it up, and it seemed to cling caressingly to his fingers. It was all he could ever have in this world of Pauline Colchester. Her "to-morrow" had come. His would come, too, by-and-by. What then? God alone knew whether his soul would ever find hers, when both should be immortal.

Will he go back again some day to Amy Minturn? Who can tell? Men have done such things. It will depend on how weary the solitary way shall seem, — how much he may long for his own fireside. At any rate, he will never tell her the story of Pauline.

THE MAN WHOSE LIFE WAS SAVED.

The Man whose Life was Saved.

I.

N a pleasant, sunshiny afternoon of early summer, Mlle. Lisa sat knitting in the door-way of a white, shining house, fronting on a silent, remote street of a garrisoned town of France, not far distant from Paris. The street was narrow and badly paved with sharp, irregular stones, sloping gradually down to a point in the centre, which formed the gutter, and at night was feebly lighted by an oil-lamp suspended to a rope and stretched across the street at the corners. The general aspect of the place was not amusing, for the habitations were few and the passers-by fewer. Long rows of high, white-washed walls, the boundaries of gentlemen's gardens, garnished with broken glass and pots of cactus, gave a certain monotony to the Rue Arc en Ciel. The very blossoms of the fruit-trees and flowering-shrubs behind the white-washed walls, looked sleepily over their barriers, as they diffused the contagious languor of their odors along the silent white street. These drowsy influences, however, seemed in no ways to diminish the carolling propensi-

ties of Mlle. Lisa, or to abate in any particular the ardor of her knitting.

Lisa Ledru was the daughter of the *proprietaire* of No. 29,— a worthy woman who had toiled to sustain herself and an agreeable, sprightly husband, addicted to no vice save that of contented idleness, through many long, weary years, and had brought up her only child, Lisa, to a point of prettiness and usefulness, which compensated for past sacrifices, and promised well for the future.

Madame Ledru's house had been for years the abode of *militaires*. She would occasionally condescend to the admission of a bourgeois, but this infringement of habit and inclination was but a condescension after all, and left her with a certain sense of degradation, when she exposed her staircase, which had creaked so long under the thundering tread of martial heel and spur, to the mild, apologetic footstep of a man of peace. Mme. Ledru's principles were well-known and properly appreciated by the regiments in garrison, and her house never lacked inmates. Her reputation for discretion and adroitness, in bringing order out of the chaotic love affairs which perpetually entangled the impetuous sons of Mars, was established on the firmest basis. No lodger was ever "at home" to an importunate creditor, so long as madame's ample person could bar the passage to their entrance, and no *tête-à-tête* of a tender nature was ever interrupted by the untimely appearance of a cherished mother or aunt, or, still worse, the jealous intrusion of a rival queen.

The court-yard of Mme. Ledru's house presented a far more lively appearance than the street in which it stood. In the centre of the court stood a large, umbrageous tree, drooping over a stone watering-trough, which gave drink to the numerous horses in the stable-yard as well as to the chickens and barn-yard fowls, who cackled and prowled about in its vicinity, as they picked up their precarious living. At times their foraging-ground would be enriched by a shower of crumbs from a friendly window above, and rumor asserted that the gallant Colonel Victor de Villeport, hero of many campaigns, with the prestige of a wound or two, and a compensating glitter of decorations, had so far abandoned himself to the pastime of chicken-feeding as to invent new methods of beguiling the monotony of the entertainment, — such as tying morsels of bread to a string and dancing it distractedly before the eyes of stupid clucking hens, until experience had taught them in a measure how to cope with this unexpected phase of their trying existence. The stable-yard, extending to the left of the court, was gay with the bright military caps of orderlies, who sang snatches of vaudeville airs, as they rubbed down their masters' steeds, and polished up their sabres and buckles.

But to return to Mlle. Lisa, who sat knitting and singing in the Porte Cochère of No. 29, on a warm summer afternoon. Her joyous refrain ceased, for a moment, as she heard the little gate opposite to the house, belonging to the Countess d'Hivry's garden, creak on its hinges, and the next instant saw protruding the round, red head of François, the gardener. This apparition, though not itself enchanting, gave Mlle. Lisa, on this occasion, the liveliest satisfaction.

"Good-morning, Monsieur François," she said, with a beaming smile, as she glanced furtively at the bouquet of flowers which was in his hand. However dull might be the instincts of François in many things, they were keen enough where Lisa was concerned; and, recognizing at once the advantages of the situation, he advanced with a profusion of bows, and a grin of ecstasy, to deposit his tribute of flowers at the feet of his *adorata.*

"What beautiful taste you have in flowers, Monsieur François," said Lisa, with a perceptible elevation of voice, and with a sidelong glance at the stone trough in the court-yard, whereat Ulysse, the orderly of Colonel de Villefort, was watering his master's horse. Mme. la Contesse d'Hivry says that she could never give a dinner-party without you to arrange flowers for the Jardinières, and to furnish all that lovely fruit for dessert, which you grow in the glass-houses.

"As to that," replied François, drawing himself up, and assuming an attitude of professional dignity, which had momentarily yielded to the all-absorbing power of Lisa's presence, "as to that, mademoiselle, I can say, without boasting, that the yellow roses and tulips of the Jardin du Roi would never be known for tulips and roses alongside of mine; though for red and white roses I will not say so much, and the pears —

"O mademoiselle! how lovely you are with those flowers in your hair!" cried out the enamored gardener, once more forgetful of his life-long enthusiasm, the pears and roses, and only mindful of the unexpected form of female seduction offered to his distracted gaze. "I never knew that roses could be so beautiful," he added, with a genuineness which would have touched any being less merciless than a girl of eighteen, bent on piquing a more indifferent admirer into something like jealousy.

"It is your roses," said Lisa, laughing, "that make me, what you call lovely. I don't make the roses. But what have you peeping out of your pocket?" she inquired, fearing that the conversation was about to assume a more tender character than she desired; "a note I should think" —

"Ah, yes! I had forgotten," said poor François, with a sigh over his own hopeless perturbation. It is from Mme. la Contesse to the Colonel de Villefort, and it was to be given without delay."

"Ulysse, Ulysse," cried Lisa, gladly availing herself of this welcome diversion, "here is a note for you."

"Do you not see, mademoiselle," said Ulysse, pettishly, not entirely pleased with François and his flowers, "do you not see that I am watering the colonel's horse? I should think, too, that the bearer of a note might deliver it himself."

François, with a soothing sense of present preferment, was about to make a good-natured reply, when the colloquy was terminated by a sonorous voice from an upper window shouting, "Ulysse!"

"*Mon colonel.*"

"Saddle one of my horses immediately."

"Impossible to use either to-day, *mon colonel;* one limps, and I have taken Mars to the blacksmith's, for he cast a shoe this morning."

"*Sapeisti!* What am I to ride then? There is the horse of Monsieur le Baron always at our service. He is a nasty, stumbling thing, but if it is very pressing" —

Victor de Villefort looked irresolutely out of the window, and twirled his blonde mustache. He was a man between thirty and forty perhaps, *distingué* in manner and bearing, and gifted with a charming sympathetic voice.

"Here is a note for you, *mon colonel,*" said Lisa, glancing reproachfully at Ulysse, as she tripped lightly across the court-yard, and passing the corridor of red brick, mounted two flights of narrow wooden stairs to the colonel's room.

"Thank you, mademoiselle," said Victor, courteously, as he took the note. "Ulysse shall stay with me always if you say so. Do the roses worn so gracefully on the left side of the head, indicate consent?"

"I wear the roses for the sake of François, the gardener of Madame la Contesse d'Hivry, who brings them to me."

"Ah! I am always allowing myself to be taken by surprise, Lisa," said Victor, opening his note and glancing over its contents. "I never keep pace with fickleness."

"But is it fickleness, *mon colonel*, to like what belongs to the Contesse d'Hivry?" inquired Lisa, lowering her eyes with assumed *naïveté*.

"For you, yes. I should say that it was. But I dare say, with your little malicious airs, mademoiselle, you mean more than that. But I advise you to wear roses on the right side for Ulysse, and then tell him that he must never leave me; and he shall not, I give you my word," said Victor, gayly, taking up his hat and gloves and moving to the door. "What a lucky thing," he continued to himself as he descended the stair-case, "that the charming countess only asks for a pedestrian cavalier! If she had asked for a mounted escort, I should have been forced to have recourse to this tiresome baron here," and Victor brushed lightly against the door of a fellow-lodger, "to have used his stumbling horse, and then to have been bored for the rest of my life, or of his life, about helping him to the cross of the Legion of Honor."

The baron in question was a retired *militaire*, who, inspired with an insatiable thirst for fame, was writing a military history of France. His chief claims to notice appeared to be the possession of a stumbling horse, and an overwhelming greed of decorations.

As Victor mused over the consequences of an incautious acceptance of the baron's steed, and over the base intrigues in which a pursuit of the coveted cross might involve him, his brow darkened, and his step grew heavier.

II.

The drawing-room of the Contesse d'Hivry was a comfortable, social-looking apartment, though with too great abandon in the matter of furniture and decorations, to claim to be a model of any particular epoch. The well-polished floors and numerous mirrors reflected back the sun's rays, which sometimes penetrated through the fragrant vines shading the windows. Bright oriental rugs were at the feet of yellow damask ottomans, and the etagères and tables were covered with rare bronzes, costly bits of porcelain, alabaster, and goblets of crystal. But the appointments of the room seemed never so complete as when the countess herself was seated in the embrasure of one of the windows, as she was on this occasion, working at her embroidery or her aquarelles. Mathilde d'Hivry enjoyed the deserved reputation of being irresistibly charming. She was nothing in excess. She was not very young, nor very rich, nor very handsome, nor very clever. But she was exactly what every one desired that she should be at the moment. No one could precisely define why they left her presence in a complacent mood and in a friendly attitude towards the whole human race. Such being the case, however, her society was naturally sought for, and reluctantly abandoned. As the countess sat this afternoon, listlessly and idly before her aquarelles, quite disinclined for work, and leaning her little head with its great coils of black braids wearily on her hands, her eyes rested mechanically on a miniature likeness near her. The miniature was that of a young man, well-featured, well dressed, well *frisé*, and well-painted. Under the sober tint of the beard and hair was the suggestion of a more fiery hue, — the red of the ancient Gaul, — just as in the mild brown eyes lurked the possibility of a flash of "*furia Francese*," the savage ferocity which centuries of civilization and good manners have only smothered in the modern Frenchman, and which shows itself any day in the blouses, as it might in the time of Charlemagne, in spite of their surroundings of millinery, cookery, hair-dressing, and the art of dancing. These reflections, however, were not in the least the source of Mathilde's preoccupation. After a prolonged contemplation of the young gentleman's miniature, she exclaimed petulantly, "Why should my aunt and uncle urge me to marry again, especially Armand?" always regarding the brown eyes of the miniature. "He looks mild enough there on ivory. But I can imagine him clothed with the authority of a husband, making scenes of jealousy, interfering, dictating, and being quite insupportable. I like him too well to expose him to such temptations. We are much better as we are. There is De Villefort. He is more solid, and more simple in character, but terribly in earnest, I should say. And they say he will never marry. Some disappointment in the past, or some hope for the future will keep him as he is,—so they say, at least;" and she fell into another revery, which was finally interrupted by a servant announcing the Colonel de Villefort.

"Oh! I am so glad that you could come to-day," said the countess, resuming her wonted gayety. "Do you share my wish for a stroll in the park this afternoon, whilst the band is playing?"

"I always share your wishes, dear countess, and am too happy when I may share your pleasures."

"That is almost a compliment, I should say, and you think yourself incapable of paying one. Why do you never pay compliments?"

"I will tell you, if you will, in return, tell me why the portrait of Monsieur Armand is always so near your favorite seat."

"The reason is, I suppose," said the countess, laughing, "that I am so used to it, that I am quite unconscious whether it is there or not."

"Then I will tell you why I rarely pay you compliments,—because I like you too well."

"So you can only compliment those whom you dislike?"

"On the contrary, those to whom I am indifferent."

"But Colonel de Villefort," exclaimed the countess, gravely tying on her white bonnet before the mirror and observing, with satisfaction, that the soft white lace brought out the lustre of her rich hair and her clear gray eyes, "do you know that public opinion decides that you will never marry?"

"Public opinion, perhaps, is wise enough to decide, because I never have married, that I never shall," replied De Villefort, offering his arm to the countess as they passed through the door.

"There is certainly a reason for such a supposition in your case, — for you have had inducements to marry." The colonel was grave and thoughtful, and, for a few moments, they walked on in silence until the sound of music roused him from a revery which Mathilde cared not to disturb. "We are in the park now," he said, at last, and almost in the midst of 'public opinion,'" he added laughing; "but, after the music, if you are not too tired for a stroll in the Jardin du Roi, I will tell you some incidents of my early life, and you shall judge whether I can marry."

"Oh! thank you," said the countess, eagerly and gratefully, more with her eyes than her voice, for the latter was quite lost in a blast of Roland à Roncevaux from the trumpets of one of the imperial bands. The afternoon being warm, the band was ranged in a circle under the protecting shade of the great, careless old trees; but the sun's rays penetrated here and there through their branches, throwing a golden light on the curls of rosy children frolicking on the green grass, casting an aureole of glory around the heads of gray-haired old men, and glittering in the epaulets of flighty young officers. There were knots of people grouped about in every direction, — French girls, by the side of their chaperons, immersed in needle-work; imperious English misses staring haughtily at the officers; ladies of opulent financial circles, in striking toilets of the last mode, fresh from Paris, and a few relics of the "*Ancienne Noblesse*," plainly attired, and looking curiously and, perhaps, disdainfully from their small exclusive *coterie*, at all this bourgeois splendor. Old women with weather-beaten, parchment faces, under neat frilled caps, were possibly retrieving, in their old age, the errors of a stormy youth, by carrying on the "*Service des chaises*." Others were plying a brisk trade among the children by the sale of cakes, plaisirs, and parlor balloons.

Joining a group of acquaintances, Victor fastidiously placed Mathilde's chair in a position sheltered from inconvenient sunlight, in proper proximity to the music, and where no dust could tarnish the hem of her floating immaculate robe. In these commonplace "*petits soins*," common enough in the life of any woman of society, Mathilde recognized a spirit of sincere devotion and protecting affection, which gave her, at the same time, a thrill of joy, and an undefined sense of apprehension and lingering regret. The Contesse d'Hivry passed, in the world's estimation, as a model of happiness, and, in one sense, she was happy. Gifted with health, a kindly, joyous nature, a due share of worldly advantages, and an easy philosophy which enabled her to accept cheerfully all daily cares and petty vexations, she was to be envied. But she had, as we all have, her own particular demon, who was fond of drawing aside a dark, impenetrable curtain, and showing her, in a vision of exceeding loveliness, the might-have-beens, and the might-be, of this deceptive life, and just as she would rush forward to seize on these delicious illusions, they would straightway vanish, leaving her to stare once more hopelessly at the same dark, impenetrable curtain. As the countess looked out beyond the great trees at the velvet sward of the Tapis Vert, at the orange-shrubs in their green boxes, at the rows of antique statues on their solitary perches, leading to the great fountain, and then the broad massive steps leading at last to the distant château, she wondered whether the little demon of "*le grand Monarque*," who had cooked in his majesty's behalf so many pleasant scenes, had ever the audacity to drop, unbidden, the dark curtain before his royal eyes. Whatever had been done, or left undone, in the case of "*le grand Monarque*," the demon had conjured up spectacles for some of his successors, which had not been so pleasant. It had not been the fate of all to look from their bed of state, with dying eyes, on the finer alleys, the shining lake, and the peaceful grandeur of the royal grounds. The curtain had been drawn once for a sleeping queen, and had revealed so dreadful a picture, that she had fled from her bed at midnight to escape it. The demon, wearied with the eternal scene of the marquis and marquise, in powder and high heels, bowing and mincing before their Great King, had chosen to vary his pleasures by calling up the old forgotten Gaul, with his red beard and his ferocious eye, to storm and rage at the château gates.

Mathilde had wandered so far away with her demon and his pictures, that she was astonished, in turning her eyes, to find Victor gazing at her with a look of troubled inquiry. The music had changed its character, and the triumphal strains of Roland à Roncevaux had given place to a plaintive melody of the Favorita, and Mathilde, glad to know her secret thoughts thus interrogated by Victor, threw them aside and became once more the gay and talkative Contesse d'Hivry.

"How gay you are now," said Victor, addressing the countess, just as the last strains of the Favorita had died away, "when I am quite the reverse. I never can listen to that duo without feeling its meaning, — from association, perhaps; for it is connected with a happy and still painful part of my life. Shall we walk now?" said Victor, as the countess made her adieus to her friends, and, taking his arm, they sauntered away to the Jardin du Roi.

"You sang that duo once," said Mathilde, half-inquiringly, "and I know more than you think of your past life, for I will tell you with whom?"

"You knew her, then?" asked Victor.

"Yes, I knew Pauline D'Arblay, slightly, but I have never seen her since her marriage, as Pauline Dusantoy."

"She is quite unchanged, at least she was when I last saw her, some years ago, and I think that she can never change," said Victor, enthusiastically. "She must always be beautiful, as she is good, and her native purity, I believe, must always resist the attacks of the world, and leave her unscathed from contamination."

"Where is she now?" asked the countess, after a few moments of silence; for in proportion to the warmth evinced by Victor in recalling these memories of the past, his companion was chilled into quiet reflections.

"In Algiers, I suppose," replied Victor, "where her husband, General Dusantoy, has been for years past."

"My enthusiasm for Pauline is only surpassed by my affection and reverence for her husband. I have known Dusantoy and have loved him from my earliest childhood, and have received from him more proofs of undeviating friendship and unwearied devotion than I can ever repay. He has saved my life, too, though he unwittingly took from me, what I believed at that time to be all that made life desirable," said Victor sadly, as they approached the palings of the Jardin Du Roi, through which the red and yellow roses and peonies, confident in their gorgeousness, were nodding their heads insolently at the *gens d'arme*, who paced listlessly before the gate. The verbenas and pansies, equally brilliant but less flaunting, were dotted about in compact groups in the parterres and on the lawn. The statue, surmounting the column in the centre of the lawn, blackened and defaced by the wear and tear of years, looked down grimly from its pedestal, as if to impose silence on all beneath. So that the jardin, in its absolute repose, found little favor in the eyes of children and nurses, who respectively chose for their gambols and their flirtations some more joyous and expansive locality. Its sole occupants on this occasion were an elderly priest, too much absorbed in his breviary to be conscious of the rustling of Mathilde's dress as she passed him, together with a pensive soldier, who possibly sought diversion from the pangs of unrequited affection by tracing with a penknife, on the stone bench which he occupied, an accurate outline of his sword.

"You knew Pauline d'Arblay as a child," said the countess to Victor, as they seated themselves on a bench at the extremity of the lawn.

"Yes, we were brought up together, — that is, our families were very intimate. She was the only child of her parents, and I was the youngest of a large family; but as my brothers and sisters were much older than myself, and Pauline was nearer my age, we were always together, and, until I was sent to college, she was my constant playmate."

"You must regard her as a sister, then," said Mathilde. "Remembrances of childish intimacy and souvenirs of soiled pinafores and soiled faces, I should think, would always be destructive of romance."

"It might be so, if the transformation of later years did not suggest other sentiments, — sentiments which, unhappily for us, were only understood when too late for our mutual happiness. I had scarcely seen Pauline since our days of hide-and-seek in the château grounds, until I finished my course at St. Cyr, and returned a sub-lieutenant, to find that Pauline, the child of the pinafore, as you say, had expanded into a lovely and lovable girl. At that age, however, I believe that few can experience a serious passion. Curiosity and inexperience of life prevent concentration on any one object, and make us incapable of estimating things at their proper value. At college, too, I had formed a romantic friendship for one of my classmates, — Dusantoy, — and the ardor of this sentiment occupied me entirely, to the exclusion of all others. Dusantoy had a rich uncle, who had purchased a large estate in the vicinity of our châteaux. He came to visit his uncle, but passed his time naturally with me. Pauline shared our walks and our drives. We read to her as she embroidered or sewed, and she sang to us in the summer twilight. We were very gay and *insouciant* in those days, little dreaming that our innocent affection would give place to a mad passion, that would one day separate us eternally, and fill our lives with unsatisfied longings. It was not until some time after, that a winter passed by us both in the gay world of Paris revealed to me the nature of my love for Pauline. A jealous fear took possession of me. Seeing her the object of universal homage and admiration induced me to declare my love. She had already discarded wealthy and brilliant suitors; and for my sake. But, alas! I was the cadet of the family, with only a good name, my sword, *et voila tout!*" Pauline's mamma was more prudent than her daughter and myself. Circumstances favored her, and separated us. I was ordered to Africa, and Pauline returned to the château; but we parted hopefully and confidently, vowing eternal constancy. When we next met, she was the wife of another man, and that man was my best friend, Dusantoy.

"*Mon pauvre ami,*" said Mathilde, almost inaudibly, and her hand unconsciously rested on his. He pressed it to his lips, and they were both silent. Victor's wound was deep as ever; but the poignancy of such a grief is already much diminished when the consoling voice of another woman and the pressure of her hand can soothe for an instant the anguish of the past.

"You know, dear Mathilde," continued Victor, "the history of Pauline's misfortunes, — the sudden death of her parents, her father's embarrassments and insolvency, and how on his death-bed he implored his only child to save the honor of his name by accepting the hand of a man in every way worthy of her, and who, at his uncle's recent death, had come into possession of an immense fortune, a portion of a Conte d'Arblay's forfeited estate. I was in Africa when the news came to me that Pauline was affianced to Dusantoy. But I heard it without a murmur; for I heard it from Dusantoy's own lips. He had been sent to Algiers on an important mission, and came to confide in me in all the rapture and ecstasy of his love. Nothing makes one so selfish and inconsiderate as an absorbing happiness. Besides, poor Dusantoy believed my love for Pauline to be purely fraternal. In my grief and despair, I believed once that I must tell him that he was robbing me of my sole treasure and hope in life; but, fortunately for him, — for us both, perhaps, for I should never have ceased to repent such an act of cowardice, — I was seized with brain fever, and for some time my life was despaired of. Meanwhile, Dusantoy, with characteristic devotion, postponed his return to France and to Pauline, that he might watch over me; and to his untiring assiduity and unceasing care I undoubtedly owe my recovery. But that is not all. Another accident befell me, which would unquestionably have proved fatal to my existence had not the skill and courage of Dusantoy again interposed to save me. At the beginning of my convalescence, when I was first able to walk a few steps in the open air, I was one day pacing the court-yard of the house where I lodged, when a low, suppressed roar struck my ear, and turning my head, I saw that a large lion had entered the open door-way, and was standing within a few paces of me. My first emotion was not that of terror, — not the same which I see on your face at this moment, *chère contesse*," said Victor, laughing; "for I recognized the animal as a tame, well-conducted lion belonging to a gentleman living in the outskirts of the city, and was about to approach him, when the sight of blood trickling from a wound in his side, and the menacing look of his eye, warned me to retreat. Escape by the outer door was impossible, as well as entrance to the house, for the lion barred the passage which led to both doors; but I thought of a gate leading to a side street, which was now my only means of flight. With feeble, tottering steps I had gained this point, and in another instant should have made my escape; but, by a singular fatality, the gate was bolted. I had neither strength to force it nor agility to scale the wall. The lion, irritated by his wound, and excited, as I found afterwards, by previous pursuit, followed me with another ominous roar and a look of hostility far from encouraging to one in my position.

"Of all that followed I have but a confused idea. I was weak and ill, — my brain reeled; but I remember that, as the lion was about to spring, a violent blow made him turn with a snarl of rage, and spring towards a new adversary, — Dusantoy, — who stood, gun in hand, in the centre of the court-yard. Then the report of a fire-arm, and I can recall nothing further. Dusantoy was an admirable shot, took cool aim, and hit the lion in the heart. Pauline and I fancied that we felt the recoil of the weapon in our own hearts for many a long day afterwards. But perhaps it was mere fancy," said Victor, lightly, as he watched the cheek of the countess growing paler as he spoke.

"To end my long story," continued Victor, "after these experiences I took a voyage to reëstablish my health; and, when I returned, I spent a week in the same house with General Dusantoy and his wife. It was heroic on my part; but I could stay no longer, and I have never seen them since. And now you understand, *chère contesse*, why I have never married."

"I understand for the past? Yes," said Mathilde, rising from her seat; "but the future"—her sentence terminated in a shrug.

The last rays of sunlight were gilding the head of the statue on the lawn; the priest had closed his book, and, with the swift, noiseless tread of his order, had glided from the garden; the melancholy soldier had girded his sword about him, after leaving its dimensions gracefully reproduced on the bench where he sat, and had followed the priest; the evening air was damp and chill, and Victor drew Mathilde's shawl around her with tender care.

"You are tired, dear Mathilde," said Victor. "You are pale; I have wearied you with my long stories, *Appuyez vous bien sur moi*," and he drew her arm through his, as they turned their steps homeward.

"You have made me so happy to-day!" said Victor, as they approached the house of the countess. "Will you give me some souvenir of this afternoon,—the ribbon that you wear?"

"We will make an exchange then," said Mathilde, laughingly, as she handed the ribbon. "I will give a ribbon for the flowers in your button-hole; and we will see who is most true to their colors."

A passionate pressure of the hand and a lingering kiss on Mathilde's primrose gloves were the only reply, and they parted. The delicate odor of the primrose gloves lingered with Victor, as he sauntered homeward in the dim twilight. The earnest, almost appealing, look of Mathilde, as he parted from her, haunted him.

"Could I ever forget and be happy?" he asked of himself. The very idea seemed to him an unpardonable infidelity, — a culpable forgetfulness of past memories, which lowered him in his own estimation. At the corner of the Rue Arc en Ciel he encountered Mlle. Lisa, hanging contentedly on the arm of Ulysse. Poor François and his flowers were forgotten at that moment, and Lisa had abandoned herself to the delights of allaying a jealousy successfully roused in the heart of the gallant Ulysse by her recent tactics.

"*Mon colonel*," said Ulysse, "a lady has called twice to see you in your absence. The last time she waited a long while in your room, and finally left a note, which she said was important and must be handed to you at once."

"A lady! Who can it be? My venerable maiden aunt, I suppose," said Victor, shrugging his shoulders, "who has lost her vicious, snarling poodle, — a wretched brute that always bites my legs, when I dare to venture them in my aunt's snuff-colored saloon, and that I am expected to find for her now, by virtue of my name of Villefort."

"The lady is young, handsome, and in widow's weeds," said Ulysse, half in reply to his colonel's muttered soliloquy, as he ran before him and vanished into the court-yard of No. 29, in search of the note.

The twilight deepened and thickened on the silent little street. The oil lamp, hanging from the rope at the corner, was lighted, but its feeble rays only penetrated a short distance, leaving the rest wrapt in mystery and gloom, and the gate opening from the Contesse d'Hivry's garden, François' portal of happiness, through which he passed into the blissful presence of his Lisa, was scarcely discernible. The evening was clear and fine, however, the stars were beginning to glimmer in the sky, and a faint band of light in the east was growing every moment into glistening silver, under the rays of the coming moon.

After parting with Victor, Mathilde entered the *salon*, and, throwing herself languidly into a chair, recalled with feminine minuteness the events and conversation of the afternoon, until oppressed with the light and warmth of the house, she sought refuge in the cool air of the *balcon*, and, leaning on the balustrade, looked dreamily through the honeysuckle vines at the parterres and lawn beyond. The meditations of the countess, however, were not exclusively romantic, in spite of the languid grace of her attitude, and the poetic abstraction of her gaze. She was fortifying herself against an attack of imprudent tenderness, by sternly picturing to herself all the practical disadvantages of a marriage of inclination. Could she incur the lasting displeasure of her aunt and uncle by marrying any one save her cousin Armand? Could she sacrifice the half of her fortune, which was the penalty of such a caprice of the heart, and sink into comparative poverty? The souvenir of a single phrase, however, in the tender inflection of a manly voice, — "*Appuyez vous bien sur moi,*" was ever present to her memory quickening the beatings of her heart, and bringing the warm blood to her cheeks. The moon had risen, pouring a flood of silver light over François' roses, and the pots of cactus on the garden-wall. The countess strolled into the garden, and, fancying that she heard a whispered conversation proceeding from the little gate leading into the Rue Arc en Ciel, she turned her footsteps in that direction.

"Is that you, Lisa?" asked the countess, rightly suspecting that the muslin dress, fluttering in the moonlight, could belong to none other than the daughter of the worthy Mme. Ledru, and that she was about to surprise a *tête-à-tête* between the coquettish Lisa, and her gardener, the enamored François.

"Yes, madame," said Lisa, "can I be of any service?"

The countess shared poor François' partiality for Lisa. Her bright eyes and shining hair were pleasant to look at, and her quick wit and cheerful voice made her a nice companion, and then she enjoyed the inestimable privilege of living in the same house with Victor de Villefort. Perhaps some bit of intelligence concerning him would escape her,—whatever it might be, Mathilde knew that it would be of thrilling interest to her. If there was to be a morning-parade the following day,

Mathilde would go to the *Terrain de Manœuvre*, to see her hero "*en grande tenue*," in the staff of the General.

"What a beautiful moonlight, Lisa! Will you walk with me towards the lake? Fetch my shawl first from the house."

"Here it is, madame," said Lisa, quite breathless, as she returned with the shawl, and wrapped it around Mathilde. François unbarred the gate and they stepped into the street.

"I should like to know, madame, what has befallen the Colonel de Villefort this evening," said Lisa, divining with tact the role she was destined to play.

"What has happened?" asked Mathilde, with ill-feigned unconcern.

"We cannot imagine, madame. But this afternoon, during the absence of Colonel de Villefort, a lady in deep mourning, young and handsome, called to see him. Finding that he was not at home, she left a note for him, and when the colonel read it, he was wild with excitement, and called to Ulysse for his horse. The horse was lame, and not fit for use, and the colonel swore, for the first time, I think since he has been in our house. That is saying a great deal for a *militaire*, madame. Ulysse has never seen the lady before. The colonel never receives any lady but his aunt the Marquise de Villefort, and that is also saying a great deal for a *militaire*, — is it not, madame?"

"Well, did he get a horse?" asked Mathilde, with a

severity which astonished Lisa, in the unconsciousness of her childish babble.

"Yes, madame; there is the horse of a queer baron, who lives with us, who often puts his horse at the disposal of Monsieur le Colonel. The horse stumbles too, but the colonel mounted him and rode off in furious haste."

"Who can she be?" asked the countess with an anxiety impossible to repress. "Did he take this direction when he rode away?"

"Yes, madame, he rode toward the lake. But take care, take care, madame!" shrieked Lisa, as the furious clatter of a horse's hoofs on the pavement warned her of danger. They had barely time to take refuge in an open door-way, before a riderless horse dashed past them.

"'Tis the baron's horse, — and the colonel, madame. *Mon Dieu! Mon Dieu!* What has become of him? Let me run for Ulysse."

"And I will go on to the lake," said the countess; "perhaps."

"Not alone, madame," exclaimed Lisa.

But the countess had already disappeared under the shadow of the houses, and Lisa, equally fleet of foot, vanished in the opposite direction, in search of Ulysse. Mathilde hurried on, — whither she knew not. A blind instinct stronger than reason warned her that delay would be fatal, and that the life, grown to be so precious in her eyes, was awaiting her coming, flickering and failing, perhaps, as it hovered near death, which was for her to avert. She redoubled her pace, and flew through the silent street, where she had passed but a few hours before leaning on Victor's arm. She saw the lake before her, calm and silvery. There was a hill to descend, and at the foot, by the side of the lake, was a loose pile of stones. She sprang forward to pick up something in the road. It was a riding-whip which she knew well and had handled a hundred times. For an instant she was motionless, her head swam, and her eyes closed to shut out the sight of a prostrate form, lying at her feet so still and calm in the white moonlight. She knew that, too. She knew well the blonde hair stained with blood, trickling from a wound near the temple; and with a wild cry for help, Mathilde raised the head, half-buried in mud and water, and gazed despairingly at the closed eyes and rigid features of Victor de Villefort.

III.

THE autumn days had come again, and the sun shone on heaps of dried brown leaves, which went whirling about in the Rue Arc en Ciel, with every gust of wind. Mlle. Lisa was in her accustomed seat in the door-way, No. 29, with shining hair and rosy cheeks, absorbed in the customary knitting, but still capable of casting sly glances in the direction whence François or Ulysse might finally appear. She was not fated to languish long in solitude, for the faithful François, never sufficiently confident of his personal attractions to present himself empty-handed before the object of his admiration, was soon standing by her side, fortified with a propitiatory offering of grapes.

"O François," exclaimed Lisa, "how glad I am to see you! Has Mme. la Contesse really gone?"

"Yes, she has gone," replied François. "Monsieur Armand and the aunt of madame have accompanied her. But you should have seen her pale face, all covered with tears. It would have made you weep, too, Mlle. Lisa, for it made me. Just think, mademoiselle, she never once tasted of the grapes that I picked for her this morning, and placed so neatly in a little basket."

And poor François groaned audibly over this conclusive proof of the countess's changed and melancholy condition.

"Ah, poor madame, she has been so ill! But why did she go, then?" asked Lisa.

"Monsieur Armand and her aunt told her that she would never get well here, and that she needed change of air, and so they hurried her away, — only giving her time to write a few lines to your colonel, whose life is not worth saving, if he cannot love Mme. la Contesse. Here is the packet for Colonel de Villefort."

"Yes, it was very brave and good of madame," said Lisa, "to find the colonel, and to pull his head out of the water. He must have suffocated, so says the doctor, if madame had not found him when she did. But there is some mystery about the handsome lady in deep mourning. I know who she is. She is the widow of General Dusantoy, who lately died in Algiers; and she came every day to inquire for Colonel de Villefort, when he was not expected to live; but since he is better, I have seen no more of her."

"Well, I will say again," said François, "that if your colonel finds the lady handsomer and better than Mme. la Contesse, then madame had better left his head in the water."

Whilst Victor and his affairs were thus discussed below-stairs with the intelligence and fairness usually developed in such discussions, he sat in his room above, pale and thin, the shadow of his former self,—twisting his blonde mustache, and gazing moodily through the window at distant hills, all brown and yellow with autumn leaves and autumn sunlight. His meditations were far from cheerful. People were perpetually saving his life. Here was a new dilemma: Pauline free once more,—free and true to her early love. Happiness once more in his grasp; but Mathilde—was not his honor half-engaged, as were his feelings a few weeks since? Could he so readily forget all that had passed between them, and all that he owed her? Could he repay the debt of his life by vapid excuses or by cold desertion? He gazed mechanically at colored prints of Abelard and Heloise, hanging side by side on the wall, and hoped that inspiration, or at least consolation, might descend on him from these victims of unhappy passion. But in Abelard's face he looked in vain for anything beyond conceited pedantry, and Heloise was too much absorbed in her own mighty resignation to trouble herself concerning the woes of others. A tap at the door roused him at last from this unprofitable contemplation, and in reply to his "*entrez*," the bright face of Mlle. Lisa appeared at the open door.

"*Bon jour*, monsieur; here is a letter from Mme. la Contesse d'Hivry, who has gone this morning with her aunt and Monsieur Armand," and Lisa paused to notice the effect of her abrupt announcement.

"Gone!" said Victor, with unfeigned astonishment. "Where has she gone?"

But Lisa observed that the hand of the colonel, as he opened the packet, was, in spite of recent illness, ominously steady, and that the surprise naturally occasioned by the news of the countess's departure was quite unmingled with the grief and despair which mademoiselle had kindly hoped to evoke. If she had dared, however, to remain until the opening of the packet, her curiosity and interest would have been rewarded by observing Victor's start of pained surprise as a faded flower fell from the open letter, and his sigh of genuine regret as the memory of the last happy day passed with Mathilde d'Hivry came to him in full force, effacing, for the moment, all trace of his recent reflections, and investing the image of Mathilde with all the poetical charm of an unattainable dream of happiness. She was no longer an obstacle in the fulfilment of his life-long hopes, — hopes persistently cherished, yet cruelly baffled. He looked wistfully at the faded flower as he crushed it in his hand, and recalled their last parting, and though the souvenirs of the day — the flower from his button-hole, and the ribbon which she had worn — had been lightly exchanged and laughingly given, he knew well that the worthless relic, which he now crumbled into dust and threw from the window, would have been tenderly kept and treasured in good faith, had his destiny so willed it. Victor turned sadly to the letter which lay before him, in Mathilde's delicate writing. It began cheerfully enough, however, as her letters were wont to do.

"I cannot leave you, dear Victor, without a word of parting, and I fear that a personal interview between invalids, like ourselves, might not conduce to our mutual recovery. In my own case, absolute change of air and scene are ordered, together with perfect quiet and rest. The one is easily gained by going to Italy; but do we ever attain the other? or would we attain it, if we could? When we next meet, for we must meet some day, *mon ami*, we shall know, by looking in each other's eyes, how obedient we have been to our physician's advice, and how great has been its efficacy. The climate of Paris will heal in your case, dear Victor, all that time has left unhealed, and I shall prepare for your coming, by making a visit of explanations as well as of adieus. Lest you find this enigmatical, I must explain, that certain rumors concerning us, so rife in our little town, have reached the ears of one who daily awaits you in Paris. I shall see Pauline Dusantoy, and dissipate all doubts, by announcing my immediate departure for Italy. I send you a faded rose-bud, which you may remember in all its freshness, and which I have no heart to throw away. But you know how jealous Armand is. Adieu, dear Victor, my hope in the future is, that the life which I have just seen trembling on the brink of eternity, may be crowned with full and perfect happiness. Adieu."

Colonel de Villefort was still weak and easily moved, and a choking sensation in the throat made him quite uncomfortable, as he placed carefully in a little drawer the letter which he had just read. He was still haunted by a wistful look of soft and winning eyes, and he seemed to hear the whispered adieu of a silvery voice, whose pure tones had so often charmed and soothed him. Is the adieu eternal? he asked himself. I think not, for I want no nobler and truer friend for my Pauline than the Contesse d'Hivry, and Pauline will hold sacred as myself the debt of gratitude due to the woman who has saved my life. But the idea of marrying Monsieur Armand! To be sure he is handsome, rich, well-connected, and has a certain charm in conversation, but quite incapable of appreciating so noble a being as Mathilde; and then what want of taste on her part! Victor's impatience was changing rapidly into indignation, at the thought of the Contesse d'Hivry presuming to marry, or trying to be happy, when another knock at the door changed the current of his thoughts. This time it was Ulysse and not Lisa who was the bearer of a letter, covered with armorial bearings, and addressed with many flourishes to Colonel de Villefort.

"What does the German baron want now?" said Victor, with an impatient shrug as he glanced at the writing, "after breaking my neck with his wretched brute of a horse? He sends many compliments of congratulation to Monsieur le Colonel for his rapid recovery after the deplorable accident, etc., etc., etc. And as he understands that Monsieur le Colonel contemplates a visit to Paris, the moment that his health permits, may Monsieur le Baron hope for his gracious intercession in his behalf, that he may at last receive the reward of merit, the much-desired cross of the Legion of Honor. Just as I supposed," said Victor, laughing. "It would save me much trouble and mental agony to give him mine, only I remember that Pauline has a weakness for these baubles."

"*Mon colonel*, may I say a word?" asked Ulysse, awkwardly, turning the door-knob to keep himself in countenance. "Mlle. Lisa"—

"Is that the word, my good Ulysse?" said Victor, waiting in vain for Ulysse to complete his sentence. I understand that you should think it the only word worth uttering, and I think you quite right. There is only poor François, who may object to have his heart broken. Lisa is a nice girl, and I have promised her that you should not leave me."

"Thank you, *Mon colonel*," said Ulysse, glowing with exultation and triumphant pride.

"Now pack my portmanteau. I shall go to Paris to-morrow in the early train."

THE ROMANCE OF A WESTERN TRIP.

The Romance of a Western Trip.

THE two following letters, received by me in the year 1852, will explain themselves.

My dear W——: When I left you at the depot in Boston, and was whirled away westward, I knew not from what point I should address you. I promised you, on the last evening that we passed together, that from time to time I would, for your delectation, give you an account of any adventure I might chance to meet with in my wanderings; as, also, to try my hand at pen-and-ink sketches of men and manners.

"Could you appreciate my surroundings, you would give me credit for a truthful adherence to my word. As to where I am at this present writing, I cannot say. In order to understand why I make so strange a statement, I must begin my story some weeks back, and narrate an incident that befell me, and led to the penning of this epistle.

"The month of May, in our northern climate, needs

no laudation as to its charms; and, after a sojourn of many years in your crowded city, I was fully prepared to appreciate all the beauty of this spring-time among the wilds of Michigan. Therefore, after leaving Detroit for the interior, I soon found (as the days were growing much warmer) that it would be wisdom for me to discard most of the luggage with which I had encumbered myself; as, by so doing, I could, as it were, cut loose from dependence upon vehicles of all descriptions; and, when my desires pointed that way, or a necessity arose, I could make use of those powers of locomotion with which nature has endowed me. Therefore, at the termination of the stage-route at H——, I selected a few indispensable articles, and, transferring them to a knapsack, sent back my trunk to an acquaintance at Detroit, with a request to hold it subject to my order, and prepared myself for rough travelling in the interior, or, as a New Englander would denominate it, 'the backwoods.'

"At the country tavern, in which I abode as a guest from Saturday until Monday, I made inquiries of the landlord as to the route I was to take, and the nature of the roads between H—— and the town of N——, which I desired to visit. My host, a shrewd, bright-eyed little man of forty, and a former resident of New Hampshire, lowered his brows, and assumed a dubious look as he listened to me; and, on my asking for an explanation of this change of countenance, informed me that, had I money of any amount about my person, I had better look to the availability of my pistols, and pay particular attention to the company I might fall in with; for, within the past two years, a number of travellers had been relieved of their possessions, and two of them murdered on the roads I should be under the necessity of passing over. The country being sparsely settled, the officers of the law had been unable to trace the perpetrators of these acts of felony. I listened to these details with much uneasiness, for, on leaving Boston, I had, by an acquaintance, been intrusted with a package of three hundred dollars, to deliver to Judge Perry, of N——, to meet some payments becoming due on a purchase of pine lands; in addition, I had upon my person some means of my own, the loss of which would indeed be a calamity of a serious nature, as I was too far away from friends to avail myself of their good services. I assumed an air of ease, however, which I was far from feeling, and left my loquacious friend, laughing defiance at all the dangers of the way. I had been unable to obtain a conveyance at anything like a reasonable rate; therefore, as the weather was so charming, had determined to undertake the journey of seventy miles on foot, trusting to obtain a ride from such travellers I might chance now and then to meet going westward. For two days, I pressed cheerfully forward, being kindly welcomed to a supper and bed in the cabin of the settlers. The roads were rough, and at places illy defined, and I was often at fault as to my route; this, and want of practice as a pedestrian, made my progress slow. As the evening of the third day drew near, I judged I must still be some twenty or twenty-five miles from my destination. I was ascending a hill over the worst road that I had yet encountered. The dwarf pine clothed the whole declivity, and rendered the approaching night more gloomy than it would have been in the more open country. I was greatly fatigued from my long day's walk, and, coming to a large boulder that had evidently rolled from the higher ground above, I seated myself to gain strength, and lifted my hat to let the wind cool my heated forehead. Down, far away to my right, I could hear the gurgling and splashing of a torrent, while the sough of the breeze among the pines made a weird music that added somewhat to a depression that had been, for the last hour, gradually stealing over me. The romantic visions I had formerly entertained of nature in her solitary moments had all departed, and I longed for the companionship of man. Some five miles back, I had been at fault as to my route; but, trusting to good fortune, had taken the road I was now upon. As I sat meditating, I all at once recollected that I had been cautioned, by a man of whom I had inquired, against taking the way that led to the hills; for, by so doing, I should go astray. Undecided as to whether it would be better to retrace my steps, or go on, in hopes of finding a lodging for the night, I had arisen, and was hesitating which way I should turn, when I heard the tramp of horses' hoofs, and down, from the higher ground on my left, rode two men.

"The obscurity had become so great while I had lingered, that I could form but an indefinite idea as to their characteristics. The foremost, mounted on a dark-bay horse, was slightly built, and evidently young. His felt hat was so slouched over his face that all I could note was, that he wore beard and mustache long, both of intense blackness.

"His companion was a much more powerful man, and sat upon the roan mare he bestrode in a careless manner; his face, also, was hidden by an equal amount of hair, and, in addition, warm as was the weather, his neck was muffled in a large woollen comforter. My presence evidently took them by surprise, for they abruptly checked their horses, and the younger man pulled sharply upon the bridle, half-turning his steed, and seemed about to retrace the way he had come, without greeting me. He, however, recovered his self-possession, and with a 'Good-evening, stranger,' continued on until he was at my side. I was truly thankful at this encounter, for I felt my doubts as to my movements would now be solved. In a few words, I stated that I had wandered from the road I should have taken, and asked their assistance to set me right. The younger man seemed to labor under restraint, and spoke but little; the other, however, offered to show me the way, and stated they were going in the direction I desired to pursue. They spoke in a manner and used language that convinced me they were men of superior culture from those one might expect to meet in the wild and sparsely settled district in which I was now travelling.

"'We have no time to spare, if we would get out of these pine-lands and beyond the river-ford before the darkness becomes troublesome,' said the larger man, as he urged his horse to a quick walk along the road up the hill. 'You had best follow me, while my companion can bring up the rear.'

"Without hesitation, I acted upon his suggestion, as I was anxious to reach a place of rest. 'You should consider yourself highly honored to be so escorted and guarded from the dangers of the road,' said my guide, as he half-turned in his saddle, with what I then thought a jocular, but have since recalled as a sinister, laugh. 'Have you any valuable property about you, that you can feel grateful for the convoy?' Without a thought of the wisdom of silence on this point, I answered: 'More than I should care or can afford to lose, for I am a thousand miles from home, and among strangers.' The next moment I felt as if I could have bitten out my tongue for its imprudence; for flashing upon me came the remembrance of the landlord's tales of robbery and violence. We had turned from the main road to the right, into a narrower track, and were descending the hill toward the river, as I judged; for each moment the noise of its waters were more audible. In a brief time after my last remark, I felt that the horseman behind me was pressing closer than was needful, and I partly stepped from the path, intending to let him pass; for I instinctively felt I would rather have them both in front. As I did so, I almost unconsciously placed my hand upon my revolver. The younger man stooped from his saddle as he came abreast of me, and, speaking in a cold, hard tone, exclaimed, 'My good fellow, we will take charge of your watch and money.' He leaned forward as he spoke, as if to grasp my collar. At the same moment he who rode in front leaped to the ground, and turned toward me. I saw my danger in an instant, and, quickly drawing my pistol, fired at the head of my nearest foe. The flash of the powder gave me a more distinct view of his face than I had yet had. As he recoiled from me, I noticed a peculiar droop of the left eyelid, and heard the expression, 'My God, I am hit!' At the same moment a crushing blow descended upon my skull, and a thousand stars seemed falling around me, and all was blackness. My return to consciousness was occasioned by a sudden contact with cold water, and I awoke to find myself struggling in the midst of a rushing torrent. Instinctively I grasped at a support, comprehending my situation in an instant. I had been hurled by my assailants into the stream we had been approaching, and they undoubtedly supposed that I was beyond the chance of recovery. The moon was not yet up, and I could discern nothing except the general outlines of the banks of the stream, which, rising high on each side, showed me I was at the bottom of a ravine. It was many minutes ere my efforts were crowned with any degree of success; at last, as I was hurled along, my hands came in contact with the drooping bough of a tree, and, weak as I was from the blow I had received and the benumbing effect of my immersion in the icy current, the principle of self-preservation enabled me to put forth almost superhuman strength, and to retain my hold on this anchor of hope.

"After many abortive attempts, I succeeded in dragging myself up, as it were out of the jaws of death, upon the rocks which composed the banks of the stream. As soon as I felt I was safe from the danger of a watery grave, my strength left me, and I fell back almost utterly devoid of life. My head felt as if a thousand trip-hammers were at work upon it; a deadly sickness came over me, and I found that I was relapsing into insensibility. By a great effort, however, I overcame this lethargy, and crawled on my hands and knees up over the piled-up rocks and bare roots of trees, until I found myself upon the soft moss and dead leaves beyond. Here I lay for a long time, slowly recovering. On an examination of my person, I found my watch and purse gone, as well as the money-belt containing the three hundred dollars in gold with which I had been intrusted. But what I felt to be a more severe loss than all else was a valuable diamond ring, that had once been my dead mother's, and given to me by her in her last illness. Some hundred and fifty dollars in bank-bills and a letter of introduction to Judge P——, placed two days before in one of my boots, had escaped the search of the highwaymen. None of my bones were broken; but a frightful swelling upon my head proved the force of the blow dealt me, evidently from the loaded handle of a riding-whip. The pain was intense, and, not knowing how serious might be the injury I had received, I determined to seek some shelter while I was yet able to do so. I cannot describe the agony I endured in the next three or four hours. Though weak and suffering, I succeeded in finding by accident a narrow by-path, or trail, leading through the forest, and continued on, shivering with cold, and frequently obliged to throw myself upon the ground, in order to gain strength and rally my wandering senses. The moon came up, and my knowledge of the time of its rising proved to me that I must have been insensible and in the hands of the two ruffians for at least two hours. I was now in a level country once more, having left the hills behind me, and, as the moon rose higher in the heavens, I could distinguish my surroundings without difficulty. I stumbled along the path I was treading, faint and ill, and at last, as I began to think I could go no further, came to a clearing, and, at my left, beheld a rough log-house among the charred stumps of the trees. I reached the door, and, after many efforts, awakened the sleepy inmates. A good-natured face greeted my sight, as a bushy head was protruded from a narrow window at my right, and a kindly voice asked, 'What is wanted?' Each instant growing fainter, I was hardly able to articulate; and, before I could explain my position, I sank insensible upon the threshold.

When I say that it is almost three weeks since that occurrence, and that from then until now I have not been in the open air, you will understand how desperate was the illness that followed. My honest host and his good wife have watched over me as if I had been a son instead of a stranger; and to their tender nursing I owe my recovery, for no physician has seen me. Far away from any settlement, upon one of the least frequented cross-roads in the wild section in which they dwell, sometimes weeks would elapse without a wayfarer passing their humble abode. Now, once more, I am able to arise and sit in the sunshine; and I hope soon to be in a condition to seek out the authors of my sufferings. As I have lain on my bed, too weak to move, I have thought much, and, strange as it may appear, I feel an innate conviction that I shall not only discover the two men who endeavored to murder me, but that I shall also recover the property I have lost. The reason that I entertain this opinion is this: The very fact of my long insensibility after the blow upon my head, and the subsequent disposal of my body by casting it into the mountain torrent, all go to confirm me in my belief that they thought me dead. Consequently, having no fear of my reappearance, they will not seek to conceal themselves, or seek refuge from detection by flight. The old lady (whom I have found a great gossip), I presume, thinks it a 'God-send' my being here; for she can now give vent to her loquacity; and, were it not that this letter was already frightfully long, I would quote some of her decidedly original remarks for your entertainment. I accounted for the plight I was in by stating that I had missed my footing in the darkness, and fallen into the stream, striking my head upon a projecting rock as I descended. At night when my host has returned from his labor, I have gleaned from him a full description of the country for miles around, and find that I can reach N—— in a day's ride, and that it is one of the most noteworthy places this side of Detroit. As soon as I dare, I shall proceed there, and my next letter will undoubtedly be mailed from that point. I shall not tell you that I wish I had remained in Boston; for to do so would be useless and foolish. I am now desirous of going forward to the accomplishment of the object I first had in view when I left you, but shall remain, however, in this part of the country, both to regain my health and strength, and to seek out and punish my assailants."

"MY DEAR W——: When I finished my last epistle, I little thought I should allow six weeks to elapse before I again took up the thread of my story; but, my mind and time have been so fully occupied, that I must crave your indulgence. It is now the latter part of July, and as you know, at this season of the year one does not feel disposed to be loquacious. That you may fully comprehend my position, however, I must be somewhat more minute in my descriptions than I could wish to be. The sun was near its setting on as lovely a day as I have ever seen, when I approached the house of which I am still an inmate. The kind-hearted man who had given me shelter and care during my illness, brought me to the village of N——, and seemed to regret parting from me. I walked up the pretty street towards a large, white house standing upon an eminence at its termination, which had been pointed out to me as the residence of Judge Perry. As I paused at a gate leading into the finely-kept grounds, I could, without an effort of the imagination, fancy that I was once more in dear New England, for all evidence of newness, seemed to have been obliterated. I turned and looked back upon the scene; the cottages quietly nestling amid a multitude of shade-trees, now clothed in their loveliest garments of green; far away the encircling hills, and, a little to my left, a pretty stream creeping down the valley, its waters turned to molten silver by the glance of the sinking sun. While lost in revery I had not noticed the approach of an elderly gentleman, who now came forward, and placed his hand upon the latch of the gate at which I was standing, at the same time greeting me with the remark of 'A delightful ending to as beautiful a day as one need wish for.' I responded, eulogizing both the weather and scenery. Whilst speaking, I took cognizance of my companion, and felt sure, from the descriptions I had received, that I was addressing the owner of the residence; and he, in answer to my inquiry, answered in the affirmative, and said, 'You are Mr. James H——, I presume. I have been expecting you for some time, having received a letter from my friend in Boston, advising me of your intention of visiting me. I heartily welcome you, and trust that on further acquaintance we shall be mutually pleased with each other; but I am keeping you here at the gate, when I should show you truer hospitality by inviting you within.' I accepted his courtesy and was soon in a pleasant bed-chamber, where I made such a toilet as my limited means afforded. As I descended the stairs in response to the summons of the supper-bell, I felt the awkwardness of my position; placed as I was, without a suitable wardrobe, in a family of such evident social standing. Trusting soon to remedy this deficiency, I entered a large apartment at the left, and found my entertainer ready to lead me to the supper-room. I made some excuses as to my appearance, which he turned off with a jest, and, opening a door, ushered me to the well-spread table. As we came forward, a young lady arose from beside an open window, where she had evidently been awaiting us, and I was introduced to my entertainer's only daughter. You have frequently bantered me on my stoical indifference to female beauty. And now, when I tell you that she whose hand I took was one of the most lovely of women, you will not have occasion to make allowance for undue enthusiasm. I shall not here attempt to describe her, further than to say, she was a blonde, with glorious eyes and a wonderful wealth of hair. Her voice was music itself, and her every movement denoted the grace of a well-bred lady. As we seated ourselves at the table, I regained my self-possession, which had been disturbed at this unexpected vision of loveliness. We chatted cheerfully as we partook of the tea and toast, and I soon felt as if with friends of long standing. When the repast ended, the daughter lovingly placed her hand on her father's arm to detain him, and my eyes encountered upon it a jewelled ring that flashed like a thing of life in the lamplight. Could I be dreaming? For an instant my brain whirled and I grew giddy, for I had discovered that which I so much prized, and had lost, — the last gift of my dead mother. This ring, from the peculiarity of its construction, and the antique setting of the stones, I could not mistake, and yet I could in no wise account for what I saw. One glance at that lovely face, whose every line spoke of innocence, was enough to drive away all suspicions as to her complicity with the men who had sought my life. I cannot detail to you the incidents of that evening; for, short as has been the time since, I have forgotten them. I was as one in a maze, and talked mechanically, and only awoke to a recollection of what courtesy demanded, when Judge Perry remarked 'that as I was evidently much fatigued, and not yet in my usual health, they would allow me to retire.' I sat at my chamber window gazing out on the moonlit valley until long after midnight, but I could illy appreciate the beauty of the scene. I was seeking to arrange some plan of action by which I might trace up this first clew to a discovery I now felt most certain. At last, wearied with fruitless thought, I determined to await the course of events, and to trust to time for additional light.

"The next few days were agreeably occupied in forming a more intimate acquaintance with Helen Perry and her father. I put forth what powers of pleasing nature has endowed me with, and my success seemed complete. Ere long I was on such terms of friendship with them as I desired; and then I learned from Helen that she had lost her mother many years before, — soon after their emigration from Eastern New York to their present home. I had thus far passed the time each day until two or three o'clock with the judge in his office, after which I wandered with Helen in the tasteful grounds surrounding her home, or upon the low-lying hills beyond. Her education had not been neglected, and her reading had been extensive. Thus we could converse upon the merits of the literature of the day, and in such topics discovered we had kindred tastes. She was ever frank and cheerful; and, short as had been our acquaintance, my heart was beginning to beat faster at her approach, and each morning, as I awoke, I looked eagerly forward to the hour that would find her disengaged from household duties, and with leisure to devote to me.

"Once or twice the judge spoke of an absent friend, a Doctor Wentworth, in a manner which caused me some uneasiness; for, as he did so, he cast upon Helen a good-natured, sly glance that meant much, and always produced a blush upon her sweet face. It was after dinner on Tuesday, that we came out upon the lawn to inspect a rose-bush, which Helen wished transplanted, when her father remarked, —

"'By the way, my dear, I received a letter from Edward this morning, and he tells me he shall be here to-day; so, as in duty bound, and like an ardent lover, I presume he will at once fly to you. I should advise that you forego your accustomed ramble, and remain at home to welcome him. I have no doubt our guest will be pleased for one day to escape the task of following you as an escort.'

"By the terrible sinking of my heart that these words occasioned, I knew in an instant that I loved her; and, half-glancing at her as I turned away (with difficulty hiding my emotion), thought I saw the bright flush upon her animated face dying away, and a deadly pallor taking its place. I dared not remain and listen to her reply, and therefore wandered on past the summer-house in which I had passed so many pleasant hours with her, until my steps were stayed upon the bank of the stream whose waters had now no music to my ears. I had heretofore been unconscious of the hopes that had gained access to my heart. Day by day I had, as it were, allowed my purposes to slumber. Her charms had bound me a willing captive, and all unwittingly I had cast aside thoughts of the future, and forgotten that the life of inaction in which I was indulging could not last. I had found ample joy and occupation in watching the play of her expressive features, and in listening to the words that came from her lips. After my first few hours of astonishment and wonder at the discovery of my stolen ring upon her hand, I had ceased, even when alone, to dwell upon the mystery connected with it. Now I was brought back to a remembrance of all I had vowed to do as I lay ill and suffering in the rude log cabin of the settler. It was long before my calmness returned, and my heart ceased to beat wildly. The afternoon had waned as I turned back towards the house and friends I had so abruptly left. It was in a more collected frame of mind that I ascended the steps, and entered the parlor. I am sure that, on encountering those there assembled, not the quiver of a muscle betrayed the agitation I felt. Helen was half-reclining upon a sofa, and leaning upon its back was the form of a tall and rather slightly-built man. She started up as I entered. Could it be that a brighter light beamed in her eyes as they encountered mine? I knew not, for the judge, who was seated near, was prompt to rise also, and said,—

"'Mr. Palmer, we are glad of your return. Both Helen and myself were beginning to fear you had been spirited away. Allow me to make you acquainted with Doctor Wentworth. Doctor Wentworth, Mr. Palmer, our guest. I trust that you will learn to value the hour that brings you together.'"

"I looked the physician full in the face, as I took his hand. The sun, streaming in through the western windows, fell full upon his features, bringing out every line in a marvellous manner, and distinctly exposing their play, as he acknowledged my greeting. The countenance was one to attract the attention, and yet not pleasant to look upon. His forehead was high and fair; hair and mustache black as night, chin smoothly shaven and dimpled, and yet the eye repelled me. As I looked at him, I had an unaccountable impression that we had met before, but I could not tell where, or why it seemed as if the circumstances attending it had been of a disagreeable nature. As, after the first words of conversational politeness, he turned to Helen, I had a few moments for reflection, and suddenly flashed upon me the recollection of the scene in the wood, — the man leaning from his horse to grasp my collar, the tones of his voice, the momentary glance I had of his face as I fired my pistol at him, and the peculiar droop of his right eye that I had noticed. Could it be possible? Had I gained one more clew to the mystery? Was the man before me the would-be assassin? No! no! I was mad to indulge such a thought. This physician, the friend of Judge Perry, a gentleman, and evidently, from the judge's own words, the accepted suitor of his daughter, could be no vulgar highwayman; and yet, as he maintained a brisk conversation with Helen, and allowed me full opportunity for close observation, the more convinced did I become that he was the man. As she raised her hand, I saw the gleam of the diamond upon it. At last the chain of evidence for me was complete. What so natural as that her lover should present this to her? I thanked God that I was to be made the instrument by which she was to be rescued from such a marriage. I forgot my own private desire for vengeance. My love for her — this beautiful and innocent girl — was of so true a nature, that every other consideration was subordinate to the one for the furtherance of her welfare. By a powerful effort I controlled my feelings, and assumed an air of ease that I could not feel.

"The doctor was all animation, and talked at a rapid rate, while I thought I had never seen Helen so dull. 'By the way, doctor,' remarked the judge, after we had left the tea-table and entered the parlor, 'have you recovered from the accident you met with a few weeks ago? Pistol-shots are anything but pleasant reminders, and you had a narrow escape.' I was gazing directly at him while the judge spoke, and for an instant, even as a summer breeze would ruffle a placid lake, a frown gathered upon his brow, and was gone. 'I am as well as I could wish to be,' was the answer, 'and have almost forgotten the occurrence.' Pleading a dull headache, I retired to my chamber at an early hour. I wished to be alone, that I might take counsel with myself as to the course I ought to pursue, in order to bring this scoundrel and his associate to justice. The longer I dwelt upon the matter, the more convinced I became that my proper course was to make the judge my confidant. He was of years' experience and discretion, and also a deeply interested party, through his daughter's connection with Wentworth.

"I slept but little that night, and was in the grounds, when my host came out for a stroll in the morning air,

I knew that it would yet be an hour before the breakfast-bell would ring; therefore, after speaking of the beauties of the morning, I took his arm as if for a promenade, and said, 'If you can spare me some thirty or forty minutes, and will come where we can by no possibility be overheard, I will tell you what I know is of vast importance to you. He looked surprised, but acceded to my request at once, recommending the arbor already in view as a desirable place for private conversation. We seated ourselves, and, with but few preliminary remarks, I gave him a full account of my adventures since leaving Detroit. He did not once interrupt me; but, as I proceeded, his face became more and more ashen, until, as I concluded by denouncing the doctor as one of my assailants, it was as white as that of a corpse.

"For a minute after I had ceased speaking he remained silent; then, drawing a long breath, he seemed to regain command over himself, and said: 'I can but believe all that you have told me, for there are many circumstances, with which you are evidently unacquainted, that go to corroborate your story. Can you remember the day of the month upon which your murder was attempted?'

"'The twenty-second,' I replied.

"'And on the twenty-fourth,' he said, 'Dr. Wentworth returned home after an absence of some days, in charge of Hugh Chapin, an intimate friend of his. He could with difficulty sit upon his horse, and was apparently suffering severely. He stated that he had been injured by the accidental discharge of his pistol, but that, as the ball had only inflicted a flesh-wound in the shoulder, it would soon heal. The explanation was plausible, and no one doubted his word.'

"'Was there any mark upon the ring by which you could identify it?'

"'On the inner-side, below the centre-stone,' I answered, 'was the letter P, in Roman characters, and above it was some fine scroll-work, and close observation would show the name of Susie, in minute lettering, amidst it; any one gazing upon it in an ordinary manner would fail to perceive it. My mother's maiden name was Susan Palmer, and this ring was presented to her by my father previous to their marriage. I feel sure that an inspection will prove my description to be true, although I have not seen the jewel since I lost it except upon your daughter's hand.'

"'I am satisfied,' said my companion; 'I have seen the initial P, as you describe it, but as it corresponded with my Helen's family name, I thought it intended for it. I can readily identify the larger of the two men, and the one who inflicted the blow that nearly cost your life, in the person of a resident of a farm-house some three miles from us, one Hugh Chapin, a bachelor and the almost inseparable companion of Dr. Wentworth. I have never been pleased with this intimacy, for I have felt an aversion to this man from my first knowledge of him. As I could give no reason for it, I have said little to Wentworth on the subject. They came here about the same time, four years ago, and Dr. W., displaying considerable skill in his profession, soon acquired a good practice, and has enjoyed the confidence of the community. This Chapin purchased the house and farm he now occupies soon after his arrival, and has always seemed to have the command of money, although I learn that he is but an indifferent farmer, and often absent from home for weeks together. I employed Dr. W. in a severe illness I had some two years ago, and after I recovered he was much at my house, and Helen saw much of him. He proposed for her hand, and at first she seemed inclined to reject his suit, but, thinking the match a desirable one, I persuaded her not to do so. I have since often fancied that perhaps I did wrong in thus using my influence, as she has since their betrothal seemed loth to accord him the privileges of an accepted lover. His profession has often called him away, but I now see it may have frequently afforded an excuse for an absence in which were performed deeds too dark even to contemplate. The sheriff of our county is a brave, shrewd man, and I will lay the facts of this case before him, and we will devise the best means of bringing these men to justice. I need not point out to you the wisdom of silence; we have cunning knaves to deal with, and must use care, so they may gain no clew to our intentions. Knowing that you had been intrusted with three hundred dollars to pay into my hands, I have wondered at your silence on the subject; but your explanation has made all plain at last. It will be difficult to dissemble in the presence of this scoundrel, Wentworth, I know;

yet for a brief time we must submit to the infliction of his presence, and allow him to visit Helen as heretofore.'

"When we returned to the house, my heart was lighter than it had been since my arrival at N——. I will pass over the record of the next few days, for nothing of importance took place. The judge and myself held frequent consultations with the sheriff in my host's office; care being taken that these meetings should attract no attention. The doctor was occupied with his patients, as the warm weather was developing disease. Once only had his confederate, Hugh Chapin, made his appearance in the village. I had seen him as he rode up the street to the door of Dr. Wentworth's office, where dismounting, and securing his horse, he entered. I would have given much to have been a private spectator of their interview, but only remained book in hand in my seat at the window. You may be sure I comprehended nothing printed upon the page before me. Not many minutes elapsed after Chapin came forth and rode away, ere the sheriff dropped in upon us. The moment he made his appearance, I saw, by the twinkle in his eye, he had pleasant intelligence to communicate. Glancing around to see that we were alone, he cast himself into a chair, giving vent to a gratified chuckle. 'We have them at last,' said he, 'thanks to the intelligence of the boy the doctor employs to wait upon him, and whom I frightened and bribed into playing the spy. A nice plot of robbery has just been concocted by the two worthies closeted up yonder. Old Seth Jones to-day received a payment upon the farm he sold Thompson, and will take it to Pollard whose place he has purchased; having to travel some twenty miles of bad road, it will be dark before he can reach his destination, and Chapin and Wentworth are intent upon relieving him of his money; the rocky gully between Harrison's and Thompson's is the point selected for operations; and I, with my men, shall take care to be there in time to have a hand in the game.'

"That was an anxious evening for me. I sat with Helen and her father until after ten, and, despite the efforts we all made, the conversation languished. I saw she felt a weight upon her that she could not cast off. As I gazed upon her face, while she bent over some feminine employment, I could perceive the great change that had been wrought in her in the few weeks I had known her. She had grown thin and pale, and a look of suffering had taken the place of one of cheerfulness. I asked myself if it could be that I had awakened her love, and that she had discovered this fact and allowed her betrothment to Wentworth to eat like a canker at her heart. I felt an almost irresistible desire to tell her how dear she was to me, and that if she returned my affection, all would be well with us. By a powerful effort, however, I choked back the words that trembled on my lips, and retired to my chamber, where I alternately paced the floor and sat by the open window until near morning. The night was intensely dark, and I could distinguish only the outline of the trees upon the lawn. It was three o'clock, and a faint streak of light began to illumine the eastern horizon, when I at last heard the tramp of horses upon the bridge that crossed the stream down the valley. I could control my impatience no longer, and, opening my door, descended the stairs with rapid feet, but the judge fully dressed was before me in the hall, proving that he, too, like myself, had impatiently awaited news of the result of the sheriff's ambuscade. We hurried down the street, and, in the dull light of the dawning day, met a party of six men having Hugh Chapin in charge. He was securely bound, and riding upon a horse in the midst of his captors. I noted the absence of Wentworth at once, and felt the most bitter disappointment, but soon learned the occasion of it. In an attempt to escape, he had been shot through the head, and was then lying dead at a farm-house near the scene of action.

"I can now condense into a few sentences what more I have to relate. On being confronted with me, Chapin made a full confession of his own and Wentworth's crime. It was he who struck me upon the head as I fired at his companion, and, after binding up Wentworth's wound, he robbed and then conveyed me to a lonely part of the stream and cast me in; my long insensibility had cheated them into the belief of my death.

"Helen made no pretext of regret at the awful judgment that had overtaken her betrothed; on the contrary, her face now wears an expression of repose which the dullest observer could not fail to perceive. Need I add that I had a long conversation with her last night during which she acknowledged her affection for me, and promised to be my wife provided her father sanctioned our wishes. The judge has since listened to my petition with a pleased smile, and answered that in due time we should be made happy.

"When our nuptials are performed, then will end my western trip and its attending romance."

THE TWO GHOSTS OF NEW LONDON TURNPIKE.

THE TWO GHOSTS

OF

NEW LONDON TURNPIKE.

THERE is a certain ancient and time-honored institution, which, in the advancement of recent discoveries and the march of modern improvements, seems destined soon to pass from the use, and then, in natural sequence, from the memories of mankind. For even the highest type of civilization is prone to ingratitude, and drops all thoughts of its best agencies as soon as it has outlived its absolute need of them. Towards this Lethean current, whose lazy waters glide so silently and yet so resistlessly along the borders of the Past, gradually undermining and crumbling away the ancient landmarks and the venerable institutions known and loved of the former generations, the whale-ships are already drifting.

For year by year, as they set sail with their hardy crews, every succeeding voyage took them nearer to the court of the Ice King, the chill of his breath grew deadlier, and the invasion of his dominions more desperate. But, lo! when Jack Tar was almost at his wit's end, a cry arose upon the prairie, and the disciples of commerce dropped their harpoons and left their nets to follow the guidance of the new revelation. Jets of oleaginous wealth sprang and spirted, and blessed was he whose dish was right-side-up in this new rain of pecuniary porridge. Instead of the old launchings and weighings of anchors, came the embarkation of all sorts and sizes of solid and fancy craft on the inviting sea of speculation, and men ran hither and thither, outrivalling the tales of the bygone voyagers, by stories of vast fortunes made in a day, and of shipwrecks as sad as any on the ocean. And so, in place of dingy casks and creaking cordage and watery perils, there sprang up the reign of pipes and drills, and for the laden ships, black and oozy with their slippery cargo, we began to have long trains of bright blue tanks speeding over all our western railways; and the whaling vessels, with their smooth, tapering sides, and blowsy crews, and complicated mysteries of rigging, seem already like forsaken hulks, hopelessly stranded upon the shores of antiquity.

But all this belongs to the Present, and any such prophecy uttered in the days with which our story has to do would have been regarded as the wildest of ravings. For then the whale-ship was a reality and a power, the terror of all mothers of wayward boys, and the general resort of reckless runaways and prodigals. The thought that it could ever be superseded by any undiscovered agency had not yet made its way into the heads of even the sage prognosticators who studied the prophets and the apocalypse, and were able to dispose of all the beasts and dragons, and to assign them appropriate places in the future, with the utmost certainty and satisfaction.

It is certain that no such forebodings startled the complacency of two young men who sat, in the gathering twilight of a mild spring evening, on a fragment of drift-wood in a little cove of New London harbor, with the waves sweeping up almost to their feet, and the western sky still flushed with the departing glory of sunset.

They were a stout, bronzed, muscular couple, loosely clad in the common sailor-suits of the period, and both with the shrewd, resolute cast of countenance that distinguished the irrepressible Yankee then no less than now. The darker of the two was the more attractive, for he had the jolly twinkling eye, and gayly infectious air that goes with the high animal temperament, and always carries a bracing tonic with it like the sea-breeze. Wherever John Avery came, all the evil spirits of dulness and mopes and blues, that conspire so fearfully for the misery of mankind, had to give way, and one burst of his spontaneous merriment would exorcise the whole uncanny troop. John was a born sailor, with all the dashing frankness, and generous, hearty temper characteristic of the class, and not deficient in the faculty for getting into scrapes that is also an invariable endowment of his prototypes.

The other was a less open face, sharper in its outlines, and with more angles than curves. Had it been less kindly, it might have been the face of a rascal, and yet an artist could easily have idealized it into that of a hero. For all these variations and contrasts of characteristic expression, that have such influence among us, are, after all, wonderfully slight affairs, and a few touches either way, upon the vast majority of faces, would give a seraph or a demon at the shortest notice. The bright, plump countenance of Jack was an open book, known and read of all men, while that of his cousin Philo was a study far more perplexing, and in the end less satisfactory. But the conversation of the two was sufficiently plain.

"Sails on Thursday, does she, Phil?" said the cheerful voice of John as his practised eye sought out a certain ship from among the crowd of vessels in the harbor.

"All hands aboard at nine o'clock's the order," replied Philo, taking off his cap, and turning his face to the wind.

"And the Sally Ann don't sail till Saturday. I say Phil, old fellow, I wish we were going together," cried John with one of his bursts.

"It's better as 'tis," said Philo, thoughtfully. "There's a better chance for one of us to come back, you know, than if we were in the same ship."

"'*Come back.*' Why, of course we shall come back, — that is, I hope so, both of us. That wasn't what I meant. I'd like you for a shipmate, — that's all," was the eager response.

"Yes, — I understand," answered Philo. "We shan't

both come home, *of course;* but there's hopes for both of us, and a pretty strong chance for one of us at least."

And then a seriousness fell upon the cousins, and for many minutes they sat and watched the tide creeping up to them like the lapping, hungry tongue of some slow monster, thinking such thoughts as will sometimes come unbidden to the heart of youth, and become more and more intrusive and importunate as we grow older.

These boys were offshoots of a sturdy Puritan stock, and the pluck and backbone of their ancestry suffered no degeneracy in them. John had been an orphan from infancy, and had grown up in an atmosphere of loving kindness and tender mercy under the auspices of his Aunt Betsy,—Philo's mother. She it was, who, in view of his orphanage, had winked at his boyish misdemeanors, indulged his naturally gay disposition in every way that her strict and somewhat barren orthodoxy allowed, and when his sea-going propensities could no longer be controlled by the mild influences of her molasses gingerbread and sweet cider, she had made him a liberal outfit of flannel shirts and blue mixed hose, and, tucking a Bible into the corner of his chest, bade him God-speed on his first voyage.

It was with some surprise that she saw him come back from a three months' cruise, with no more serious damage than a scar across his forehead; but still she felt reproached at the sight of it, and on Jack's next start rectified her previous neglect, by sending Philo along with him in the capacity of mentor and protector,—an office which she, in the devotion of her heart, would most joyfully have undertaken herself if the art and practice of navigation could have been adapted so as to admit of the services of an elderly lady. But becoming convinced of the utter impracticability of this plan, she wisely settled herself down to be comfortable with tea-drinking and knitting-work, with great confidence in Philo's sobriety and force of character, as applied to preserve her darling Jack from harm; for Aunt Betsy, like many other excellent people, was not free from favoritism, and her adopted son was the child of her affections, while Philo had the secondary place, and was expected to consider it his highest happiness to fiddle for Jack's dancing, and otherwise to hold the candle in a general way for the benefit and pleasure of that superior being. Had Jack been less jolly and generous, or Philo less amiable and forbearing, this maternal arrangement would have been a fruitful source of jealousy and contention; but the two natures were so fortunately balanced that even the one-sided weight of Aunt Betsy's partiality worked no such derangement of the family peace, as might have been supposed. The boys had made three short voyages together, and were now about shipping for their first long absence in different vessels only because Philo's superior education and business aptitude qualified him for the position of supercargo, which had been offered him on board the Skylark.

Philo was already developing the great Yankee trait of penny-catching, for even then he had saved quite a pretty sum out of the very moderate pay of a foremast man in those times, and this, in addition to his patrimonial inheritance of a few hundred dollars, made a nice nest-egg for the fortune that he hoped to realize in late life. Jack, too, had his property interest, for he had just come to man's estate in the eye of the law, and his little property, carefully hoarded, and with its due interest had been, only the day previous, paid into his hands in good gold, accompanied by much sound advice and the warmest good wishes from his benignant guardian, 'Squire Tupper, who, thanks to Aunt Betsy's interposition had found him the most dutiful and least troublesome of wards.

Philo renewed the conversation by inquiring whether Jack had thought of any particular mode of investment, and stating his own intention of purchasing an interest in the Skylark, if on his return it should appear advisable. But the former topic appeared to push itself uneasily uppermost, and he soon came abruptly back to it, —

"I shall do that thing if I live to see home again; and, if anything should happen that I don't, I want my money to go to you, Jack, except half the income, and that I want to have settled on mother as long as she lives."

"You'd better say all the income, and the principal too, for that matter, Phil," cried the hearty Jack, with a little break in his voice at the last words.

"No," replied the cousin, soberly. "There's enough

besides to keep the old lady comfortable as long as she lives, and more would only worry her. If she gets something to show that I didn't forget her, it'll be better than if she had it all to take care of; and she'll be just as well suited to have it go to you."

"But think of my getting what Aunt Betsy ought to have," remonstrated Jack, sturdily.

"It's best," said Philo.

"And to hear you talk as if you was bound straight for Davy Jones' locker," pursued Jack.

"I shan't go any straighter for talking about it, as I know of," answered Philo, looking steadily towards the dim horizon as if his fate lay somewhere between the water and the sky.

"Well, then," shouted the impulsive Jack, "if it must be so, I'm glad I can match you at the other end of the same rope. You're as likely to come home as I am, and, if I'm never heard from, all I've got shall go to you."

"Then we'd better make our wills in form, if that's your wish," said Philo, rising from the log.

"We'll make all fast to-morrow," remarked Jack, cheerfully; "though it makes one feel queer to be doing such business at our age."

"It can't hurt anything; and we're no more likely to meet with bad luck for having things in ship-shape," replied Philo, as they walked up towards the little town, whose twinkling lights winked like fireflies out of the darkness.

"Let's do it to-night, and have it over," exclaimed Jack, who found an unpleasant creeping sensation gaining upon him as he dwelt on the subject.

"Well," said Philo.

The cousins turned into the main street of the village, now a busy mart of business, but in those days broad and grassy, with a row of respectable gambrel-roofed houses, each with its liberal garden at the side. Pre-eminent in respectability was the abode of 'Squire Tupper, with its large, clean yard, small, patchwork-looking windows, and ponderous brass knocker, which disclosed the terrific head of some nondescript animal in most menacing attitude. Upon this brazen effigy Jack sounded a vigorous rap, since 'Squire Tupper was the prime magnate and authority of the small town, in all matters requiring legal adjustment; and any well-instructed resident would as soon have thought of having a funeral without the minister as of making a will without the advice of the 'squire.

The summons was answered by a pretty blonde girl, dressed in the nicest of blue stuff gowns, the whitest of muslin tuckers, and with her pretty feet displayed to advantage by fine clocked stockings and neat morocco shoes. All these little matters and her dainty air gave her the appearance of a petted kitten, or, rather, of some small, ornamental image, made of cream candy, and kept in a Chinese doll-house.

She turned rosy at sight of Jack, who came instantly out of his solemn mood, and, in the frank, saucy way habitual to him, swung his arm around the neat waist, and, spite of some tiny remonstrances and vain struggles, planted a big sailor kiss right in the centre of the demure mouth. All this was natural enough; for, besides being the 'squire's ward and connected in that sort of cousinhood which extends to the forty-ninth degree of consanguinity, Jack had now regularly "kept company" with Molly for several months, and all his Sunday nights on shore were piously devoted to "settin' up" with her in the prim, sanded best parlor, where it is not to be supposed that he abstained totally from such "refreshment" as Mr. Sam Weller was accustomed to indulge when opportunity offered.

But his demonstrativeness served to discompose Molly's ladyhood on this occasion; and the presence of Philo with his business-like face added so much scandal that she disengaged herself as quickly as possible from Jack's audacious grasp, and, with such dignity as a white kitten might assume in the presence of two intrusive pups, ushered them into the family "keepin'-room," and withdrew, as if she wished it understood that she washed her hands of them and their kind from that time forth. But Jack slipped out after her, and probably made peace; for they returned together, — he very brisk and shining, and she blushing like Aurora.

Philo, however, meant business, and said as much in plain terms, that set Miss Molly into a perfect maze of conjecture as she went to call the 'squire. Her only solution of the mystery was that Jack had now come for the momentous *pop*, toward which events had been tending; and that Philo had accompanied him in the character of second. She felt a little piqued that she had not been able to bring him to the point herself; but then it was certainly very straightforward in him to come right to her father in that way; and so the little lady rushed out to the wood-pile in a perfect flutter of delicious perplexity, and imparted the fact that the two young men had called *on business*, with such decided emphasis that the 'squire immediately took the cue, and prepared himself to be especially benignant and paternal.

Relieved of Molly's inspiring presence, Jack felt all the solemnity of the affair returning upon him, and, as is usual with these strong, mercurial natures, it loomed before him more and more grim and ghastly, till, by the time that the 'squire made his appearance, he had become almost persuaded that his last hour was really approaching. This state of mind imparted to his countenance an expression of such touching melancholy as made the old gentleman take him for the most despairing of lovers, and wrought upon his sympathies amazingly.

'Squire Tupper was the embodiment of magisterial dignity, owlish wisdom, and universal benevolence. With a fine, showy person that was in itself the guaranty of unimpeachable respectability, he had gone on in life, and come to hold the position of an oracle; not on account of anything he ever said, but because of a general way that he had of looking as if he could on all occasions say a great deal if he chose, which is a sure way to attain the distinction of being considered remarkably well-informed, though it is one that is greatly neglected of late years. The world laughs at witty people, and despises them; and 'Squire Tupper was a bright example of the truth that it takes a thoroughly dull man to be profoundly respected.

He now saluted the cousins with grave urbanity, and deliberately placed his stately form in the arm-chair, taking a fresh cut of tobacco as a preliminary to business. If Molly had enough of mother Eve about her to cause her to peep and listen behind the door, we don't know as it concerns us. We don't say she did; but would be slow to take the responsibility of declaring that she didn't. Young ladies, who may chance to peruse this veracious history, are at liberty to decide this point according to their own estimate of the temptation, and the average feminine power of resistance.

Jack plunged desperately into the middle of the subject, and then tried to swim out toward the introduction.

"We thought we'd stop in, sir, this evening, as we've made up our minds to do a certain thing; and it seemed as if we — I mean I — felt as if I should like to have it done, and over with."

"I see, I see," replied the 'squire, with the utmost consideration for Jack's embarrassment, and the delicate nature of his errand. "You've spoken to Molly about it, I suppose?" he added, encouragingly.

"Why, no. Didn't think it was worth while, as you was at home," answered Jack.

"Ah, I see! Jes' so, jes' so! Very thoughtful in you, Jack, — very, indeed." The 'squire paused, and took a pinch of snuff, nodding his satisfaction, and proceeded: "It's highly gratifying to me, Jack, to see you so thoughtful as to come to me first on this business; though it isn't what all young men would do. I'm glad to see that you respect the parental relation, and respect my feelings, though you've no parents of your own; still you've had an excellent bringing up by your Aunt Betsy, and I've tried, in my humble way, to do what I could." (Graceful self-abasement was one of the 'squire's strong points.) "And now I say you've acted just right, because I am better capable of judging what is for Molly's good than she can be herself; and, of course, I'm the person to be first consulted; and it's most creditable and gratifying" —

"Why, it isn't about Molly, at all!" cried Jack in bewilderment.

O happy, doting pride of fatherhood! What a falling off was there, and what blankness, followed by confusion, overspread 'Squire Tupper's countenance, as the nature of his blunder and its extreme awkwardness became apparent to his puzzled faculties.

"No — no — certainly not — not in the least!" gasped he, catching after his dignity, as a man drowning grasps at straws.

"We came to see if you could attend to making out our wills, this evening," said Philo.

The 'squire looked from one to the other with such

dazed incredulity that both the young men applied themselves to explanations which brought his senses back into the world of facts.

"Yes, yes, certainly, — very creditable and prudent in you to wish to make things all snug before you go. Excellent idea; though you're both rather youngish to be doing such business. Still it's highly gratifying to see you take it up in this way, — certainly, — just let me get the materials." And the 'squire plunged with great eagerness into the subject, briskly opening an old-fashioned secretary, and setting out upon the table a heavy stone inkstand, a sand-box, some large sheets of paper, and a bunch of quills; and then, being quite restored to his accustomed equilibrium, begged them in the most impressive magisterial manner, to state their wishes, and commenced making his pen, while Philo explained the subject-matter of the conversation previously recorded.

"I see, I see!" said the 'squire, deliberately, when he had elaborated the point of the quill, and tried it repeatedly on his thumb-nail. And, without further ado, he drew his chair to the table, and headed the page in a large, round hand: "*The Last Will and Testament of Philo Avery;*" following it up with the regular formula for such cases made and provided.

"*In the name of God, Amen.*

"I, Philo Avery, of the town of New London and state of Connecticut, being of sound mind and memory, and considering the uncertainty of this frail and transitory life, do, therefore, make, advise, publish, and declare this to be my last will and testament," etc.

Scratch — scratch, went the 'squire's pen, interrupted only by occasional dips into the ink, while the two testators sat and looked on in unwinking silence, and the tall candles flared and sputtered as their sooty wicks dropped down into the tallow. Hardly had this happened when Molly tripped shyly into the room, bringing a pair of silver snuffers on a little tray, and with one dexterous nip relieved each smoking luminary of its incumbrance, at the same moment casting her demure eyes upon the page which her father was now covering with sand. If she was not ignorant of the old gentleman's palpable blunder (and remember the narrator takes no responsibility on that point), she was certainly very innocent and unconscious, and, as Jack looked at her, he anathematized his own stupidity in not taking the opportunity which the 'squire had so temptingly opened for him, and determined that he would rectify the omission speedily.

Meanwhile, the quill travelled over another broad page, and the documents were ready for the signatures. And then it was necessary that Molly and the hired-man should be called in as witnesses, and the former made very wide eyes of wonderment (little budget of deceit !) when she learned the nature of the papers, and wrote her name in a tiny, cramped hand, with many little quirks like the legs of spiders, and this was supplemented by the laborious autograph of Silas Plumb, the teamster, a young man of limited education and bushy hair.

And when all this was done, the cousins exchanged

the wills, and tucked them into their respective side-pockets, feeling greatly relieved, and the 'squire, after receiving his fee in a benevolent, deprecating manner, as if it was quite a trial to his feelings, but must be undergone as a duty, brought out some excellent port wine, and pledged them both in liberal glasses, with wishes for their prosperous voyage and safe return. And at the mention of this sorrowful topic, poor Molly's spirits suffered such charming timid depression, and were affected to such a degree that when Philo took leave, it was necessary for Jack to lag behind, and finally allow him to go away alone, since nothing else would serve to restore the languishing damsel to comparative cheerfulness. At this interval of time, and without the advantage of being an eye-witness, it would be a vain attempt for anybody to undertake a minute account of how, standing in the low "stoop," with its little round posts like drumsticks, and huge tubs of thrifty, rough-leaved plants, Molly made herself perfectly irresistible with her shy regrets, and how, when her grief and apprehension at once welled up from her heart to her face, in the midst of bashful palpitations and broken sobs, her proud little head wilted weakly over on Jack's shoulder, and she begged him not to go sail-ail-ailing away, and be drownd-ed-ed — and have that horrid old will-ill-ill for his sole memento. Neither would it be easy to portray how Jack soothed and petted, with all the little endearments that are such delightful realities for the moment, but so silly and absurd to remember, and finally, when nothing else would answer, committed himself past all remedy, as what man could help doing, with such a dainty little figure leaning close, and the sweetest of mournful faces buried in his collar. And then, there were more tears and kisses, and at the end a long, quiet talk of all that should be realized when that one voyage was over, and he should be ready to resign his sea-faring life.

At last Jack tore himself away from all these enchantments, and rushed home for a couple of hours of delicious dreamy tumbling about in bed before daylight, which seemed to come much sooner than he had calculated, and aroused him to complete his preparations for departure.

Everybody knows what a queer, altered aspect certain actions and feelings take after one night, and the dawning of the clear, practical light of the next day. Ideas that have seemed most urgent and actual will at such times appear extremely unreal and visionary, and be quite eclipsed in interest by the trifles that come in between and demand immediate attention. Jack found it so, in the hurry and bustle of the next day, what with the preparations for sailing, and all the little matters that such a start involves. The doings of the previous night seemed quite distant and foreign to his own personality; and it needed the big-folded document, with its formal phraseology and crisp rattle, to convince him that the acts of the evening before had not been a rather memorable dream. Once, in the course of the day, he took out the will, read it hastily over, and then tucked it away in a little brass-bound box, that answered for him the same purpose that a Herring's Patent does for prudent young men of the present day.

But however it might be about the wills, and the chances that the Great Reaper should overtake either of the cousins before the return-voyage, Molly was a present and delightful reality; and that very evening Jack made her another visit, justified 'Squire Tupper's presumption of the former occasion, and amid Molly's tears and kisses, and big sighs and little sobs, wished most heartily that the Sally Ann had made her cruise, and that the future programme was ready to be carried into effect. But then, he might be lucky enough to pay for waiting; and if anything should happen to Philo in the interval, — of course, he hoped there wouldn't, poor fellow; but accidents will happen, and if anything so sad should occur, why, then he would be in a position to keep Molly in the style she deserved and was accustomed to; and to buy out a share in some nice little craft, that should bring home to them treasures as rich, after their kind, as those that the ships of Tarshish brought to King Solomon. But all this was mere conjecture, and Jack renounced it with a feeling of reproach for having indulged it even for a moment.

The next day the Skylark sailed, Philo starting away from the old house with his chest on a wheelbarrow, and leaving Aunt Betsy on the door-step, with her lips pressed very tight, and all the grim fatalism of her religious faith making stern struggle against the natural motherly instincts of her heart. For she did love Philo; and even the reflection that he wasn't going to wait upon Jack, according to his established usage, was lost in genuine grief for his departure.

Jack rowed out to the ship with him; and it would be doing both an injustice to ask whether the cordial regrets of their separation were mingled with any remembrance on the part of either, that in case they should never meet again, one of them would be a few hundred dollars richer for the death of the other.

On the morning of May 5th, 1805, the Sally Ann sailed out of New London harbor. On the evening of September 12th, 1808, she dropped anchor in the very spot which she had left three years and four months before.

The first object, aside from the familiar shore, that met Jack's recognition, as they sailed up the bay, was the ship Skylark, arrived just six weeks previously, and the first man he saw, as he stepped on land, was his Cousin Philo. There could hardly have been a more cordial greeting than that which the bystanders witnessed; and yet a close look into the heart of each might have disclosed a shade of something strangely inconsistent with the outward semblance of happiness that both wore.

For three years is a long time for some thoughts and impulses to mature in, and day after day out at sea, with only the monotony of the ever-undulating waves, and the easily exhausted resources of variety to be found on shipboard, give great opportunity for brooding, and such speculations as come naturally to people who are idle and isolated. Seeds of the devil's planting possess a peculiarly vital and fructifying property and are sure to come to maturity sooner or later. One can easily imagine the thoughts that might have come to these two young men in the long, solitary watches, come perhaps like suggestions from the world outside, wafted on the wings of the wind, or caught up in chance hints and scraps of sailor talk, but coming nevertheless straight from the God of mammon, and, with their slow canker working a steady and sure corruption. And yet, neither had probably ever allowed these thoughts to take any such positive form as to be capable of recognition. They were always, even in the moments of their strongest domination, veiled in some perfectly innocent mental expression, such as *if* anything should happen, or *supposing* such an affliction, — meditations which the most sensitive conscience could not possibly challenge, but which had a way of creeping in upon the minds of these two far oftener than they would have done, but for the existence of the wills.

Philo had an inborn love of lucre that was strong enough to give spice and fascination to these ponderings of possibilities, while Jack was constantly under the stimulus of his fondness for Molly, and desire to make a handsome provision for her. And by these means, this indefinite *if*, acknowledged at first only as a remote and dreaded contingency, gradually took to itself substance, and began to figure in the plans and projects of each as if it were almost a positive certainty. Always, however, with the proviso that it was a very sad possibility, to be devoutly deplored and hoped against, but still accepted and treated as an actuality. And such an effectual devil-trap did this *if* prove to be, that this meeting of the two cousins was, in the hidden consciousness of each, in the nature of an unexpected shock that made a sudden scattering of many schemes and purposes, all based, to a great extent upon that wicked and fallacious *if*. And while all this was lurking under the demonstrative warmth and gladness of their greeting, probably no greater surprise nor horror could have befallen either than to have had the veil of his self-deception for one moment lifted, and to have had a single glimpse at the truth within him, or a single intimation of the lives that they two should lead through the next half century under the evil consciousness of that ever impending *if*.

But nothing of this supernatural character befell them, and after a few warm greetings among the crowd on the pier, Jack hastened toward the town. There were some changes in the familiar streets; buildings newly built or altered, signs changed, and a barber's pole freshly painted. All these he observed carefully as he walked on. When he came in sight of 'Squire Tupper's, the radiant, blushing face of Molly disclosed itself for an instant at the window, and speedily reappeared in a flutter of delicious expectancy at the half-open door, for the news of the arrival was already all over town. She gave a series of little screams as Jack, with such a big black beard, and so very brown, came up and saluted her with a strong bearish hug and a general smell of whale-oil.

For Jack was considerably altered by reason of a certain manly reticence that seemed to have grown on with his whiskers, in place of the old boyish dash and frankness. Molly had become steady and womanly, too, and now saw with vast pride the dignified way in which Jack deported himself, how he met the 'squire's gracious welcome with equal ease and affability, and talked of his voyage and its adventures in such a quiet, modest way as showed him to be every inch a hero. And when, after a short stay, he spoke of Aunt Betsy, and would not prolong her waiting, Molly was quite resigned to let him go, contenting herself with dwelling upon his improved looks, and indulging in charming little maidenly reveries that centred in the anticipated joys and splendors of a certain day which she had settled in her own mind as not far distant. — Alas, Molly! Indulge your reveries, poor girl. Dream on, and let your dreams be sweet. Play over and over in anticipation your pretty little drama of white dresses and bridesmaids and wedding-cake, and make it all as gay as possible, for little else shall you have by way of reward for your many months of constancy to Jack Avery, save his occasional attentions and the satisfaction of being for years the wonder and mystery of all the gossips in town. Yes;

for years. It may as well be said now as any other time. The day when Molly's dreams should be realized withdrew itself from time to time, and at length took up its permanent position in the distant horizon of uncertainty. "Colts grew horses, beards turned gray," but Molly Tupper was not merged in Molly Avery, and there were no prospects of that consummation more than had appeared for the last — well — we wont say how many years. For tender and devoted as Jack was for a long time, there was a change in him, that brought something of constraint and reserve between them, and, with all her delicate feminine tact, she could never lead him into any direct avowal of his wishes on the subject. And since Molly was the very paragon of maidenly modesty and trusting devotion, she came to indulge the conviction that Jack knew best, and had some wise though inscrutable reason for delaying matters. And in time, even those indefatigables, the village gossips, wearied of wondering and surmising, at their perennial tea-parties, and the whole thing settled down into a discouraging calm.

And yet Jack had no design of doing an injustice. He was really fond of Molly, and fully intended to marry her. But for that ever-present *if*, and the complications it involved, the event would have taken place in due time. His reflections sometimes took a very painful turn, as he pondered the subject. Here was this beautiful, affectionate girl, to whom he had long been pledged, waiting his time with all the truth and constancy of her loving nature. And here he was, living a dreary and almost hopeless bachelor life, and standing in the way of any advantageous match which might be otherwise open for her acceptance. But, in case of his marriage, the will arrangement must be broken up, and he should have the mortification of making that suggestion to Philo; which seemed an almost impossible thing to do, for not a word with reference to it had ever passed the lips of either since the night when the agreement was made, and both had come to regard it with something like a superstitious dread, as a theme whose discussion might portend some fatal result.

And then, again, thought Jack, life was such an uncertainty, and a few months of waiting might make a vast difference. Suppose, in his foolish haste, he should throw up the will arrangement, and marry Molly, and it should turn out, after all, that a little delay would have improved their condition so much. Though life insurance was still unknown, and its cool calculations and scientific averages would have been then regarded as the extreme of impiety, and its risks as a wicked tempting of Providence, Jack had made out in his own mind a tolerably accurate table of averages, which showed quite conclusively against his cousin's chances for longevity. It is hardly to be supposed that Philo had neglected the same satisfactory proceeding, or that his results were very different.

And thus this corrupting temptation, that is the root of all evil, had crept upon these two noble young hearts distorting and defiling them with its slow taint. And even now, either of them might truthfully have questioned, —

> " What shall I be at fifty,
> If nature keeps me alive,
> If life is so cold and bitter,
> When I am but twenty-five ? "

It would be too dreary a task to follow them year by year. Let us make leaps and take glimpses at them by intervals.

Twenty-five. What we have seen.

Thirty. Aunt Betsy, weak and childish for many months, has gone to her long home, with a final admonition to Philo that he must make Jack the object of his best watch and care for the entire period of his natural life.

Molly is still pretty, though a little thin and with a perceptible sharpening of the elbows. Her color is not quite so high, nor her figure so plump. She keeps house for the 'squire, with devotion and good management that are the admiration of the town; continues to love and trust in Jack with unabated fervor, though some young women, whom she remembers to have held in her arms when they were babies in long clothes, are long since married and have babies of their own. Still she receives the sometime visits of her laggard lover with the same grace and sweetness, confident that it will all come right in time; has dropped the old familiar

"Jack" for "John" or "Mr. Avery," which is a hint that we ought to do so, too.

That unfathomable individual has been for some time a partner in a grocery establishment, carrying on a good business, and realizing fair profits; devotes much of his leisure to revising the imaginary insurance table, and has brought it down considerably closer; maintains a great regard for his Cousin Philo, and has much affectionate solicitude for his health; gives occasionally to various benevolent objects; is extremely regular in all his habits, and is generally regarded as a very nice young man, who has turned out much better than was expected of him.

Philo has purchased a farm in an adjoining town, and is improving it with great care; is considered rather "near" in his dealings, and is generally quite distant and reserved. Suspicions are entertained that he has been disappointed in love, though nobody pretends to know the particulars; always takes a great interest in his Cousin John, whom he suspects of a tendency to dropsy. John, on his part, thinks Philo consumptive.

Thirty-five. No great variation.

Both the farmer and the grocery-man are moderately prosperous; though neither ventures much into speculation, because each is mindful of possibilities in the future that will give great additional advantages. The insurance table has been reduced to one of the exact sciences.

Molly, poor girl, has faded a shade or two. She still keeps house, and raises an annual crop of old-maid pinks and pathetic-looking pansies, together with sage and rosemary and sweet marjoram, which she dries and puts in her closets and drawers, in order that their delicate, homelike fragrance may keep out the moths and pervade her apparel. But, as she moves so briskly and cheerfully about her little tasks, or bends over some bit of sewing or other ladycraft, grave doubts intrude themselves; and, if she were one whit less patient and self-forgetful, she would sometimes throw aside all these little occupations, and, like Jephthah's daughter, bewail her virginity. And, as she sits on Sunday mornings in church, alone in the pew except the 'squire, — now an old man who takes incredible quantities of snuff and drops the hymn-book, — as she sits thus, and watches the happy matrons, no older than she, coming in one by one, with their manly husbands and groups of rosy children, there comes up, sometimes, a great rising in her throat, which she is fain to subdue by taking bits of her own preserved flag-root, which she carries always in her pocket. Or, when she sees some pretty bride arrayed in the customary fineries, she sighs a little, as the thought that she has lost her best bloom comes uneasily to the surface; and then she sometimes looks timidly around to see if Mr. Avery has come to church. But Mr. Avery isn't often there; the insurance table takes up a good deal of his attention on Sundays.

Molly has long ceased to dream about the white dresses and orange-blossoms. She would be glad, indeed, to make sure of a plain dark silk and only two kinds of cake; and of late even her hopes of these have become empty and melancholy as a last-year's birds-nest. Yet she clings still to the shadow of her old coquette girlhood, and rejuvenates herself with a new bonnet every spring, with as much seeming cheerfulness and confidence as if she were fifteen instead of thirty-five.

Forty. Decided changes.

'Squire Tupper rests in a grave marked by the most upright and respectable of tombstones. And then all the chattering tongues, that had before wagged themselves weary with gossip and conjecture, took a renewed impetus, and it was settled in all quarters that Molly would now be married as speedily as the proprieties of mourning would permit. And John himself, it would seem, thought as much; for, without any undue haste, he did make some motions looking that way. He bought a new gig, and took Molly out to ride several times, besides sitting very regularly in her pew at church. And, having thus evinced the earnestness of his intentions, he made himself spruce one Sabbath evening, and proceeded to call on her, with the express design of asking her to fix the long-deferred day.

But what was his surprise on finding, as he came upon the stoop where he and Molly had so often exchanged vows of eternal fidelity (which had, indeed, been tolerably tested), the best parlor gayly alight as in the days of his early courtship, and to hear a male voice in very animated conversation with Molly.

Curiosity and pride alike forbade him to retreat; but how was his surprise intensified to dismay when Molly, looking remarkably bright and young, ushered him into the presence of Mr. Niles, a most respectable gentleman resident in town, whose wife had been now three months dead. He was as smiling and interesting as Molly. And presently that outrageous damsel spoke up in the easiest way in the world, —

"You dropped in just the right time, *Cousin* John, for now you shall be the first one to be invited to our wedding. It is to come off a week from next Wednesday in the evening. We have just settled the time, and I shall have to stir around pretty lively to get ready."

It was all true, and there was no help for it. John Avery had presumed a trifle too much upon the elastic quality of Molly's love for him, and now, at the eleventh hour, her seraphic patience had given way, and let him most decidedly and disgracefully down. When her father was dead and she left in loneliness, and John still delayed to make direct provision for altering the state of things, Molly felt that she had passed the limit of forbearance, and with a sudden dash of spirit, in which she seemed to concentrate all the unspoken pain and suppressed sense of wrong that had struggled in her heart through all these years past, she actually set her cap for this forlorn widower with six children, caught him, rushed him through a violent courtship, evoked from his stricken heart an ardent and desperate declaration, accepted, and married him, all in the space of eight weeks.

And this was John's first intimation. Will any woman blame her if she *had* been a little studious to conceal the preliminaries from him, till it should be time to acquaint him with the result, or if she wasn't especially tender of his nervous sensibilities in making her disclosure?

But he was bidden to the wedding, and must needs go, — which he did, looking very glum, and kissing the bride with far less gusto than he had done in former times. But it was a very festive occasion, notwithstanding, for the bridegroom appeared in a blue coat with brass buttons, and his hair was greased to preternatural glossiness, while all the six children stood in a row, their stature being graduated like a flight of steps, and the cake was all that Molly had ever pictured it in the wildest flight of her imagination. And Molly herself in a perfect cloud of gauze and blaze of blushes renewed her youth prodigiously.

It was all over, and John Avery walked slowly homeward with a glimmering consciousness that the things of this life in general were rather shaky and uncertain, — indulging even a brief doubt as to the reliability of his system of averages.

Fifty. Both of our old bachelors are beginning to

grow gray and morose. Philo stoops considerably, but is otherwise in excellent physical preservation; reads all the medical books about abstinence and frugality as the means of promoting long life, and practises rigidly upon their principles. John is equally tough and temperate. Neither shows the least sign of giving out for fifty years to come. Both have increased in substance and have the reputation of being "forehanded." The insurance table has been reduced to the very last fraction; but, spite of its scientific accuracy, seems to be one of those rules that are proved by their exceptions.

Mrs. Niles is the most devoted of wives, the perfection of step-mothers, and rejoices, besides, in a chubby little boy of her own. All the seven are united in neglecting no opportunity to rise up and call her blessed.

Sixty. Ditto — only more so.

Seventy. The Ghosts?

Yes, indulgent reader, your patience hath had its perfect work, if it hath brought you through all these preceding pages, in order that you may witness this *denouement* scene, in which the ghosts appear, with such real and startling semblance in the eyes of some of our actors, that, in comparison, the fifth act of a sensation drama would have seemed mild as milk.

It is to see these supernatural visitants that we have brought you all this long road. Let them show themselves but once, and we will then be content, nay glad, to drop our curtain, retire from the footlights, and whisk our actors back to the serene shades of private life. Grant us, for a little time, the gifts of conjurers and "meejums." Let our Asmodeus take you in charge, and show you things that are beyond the range of mere mortal perception. Ubiquity shall be yours while you journey into the land of spirits, and the name of the mischievous wizard and terrible practical joker who conducts you thither shall be Jack Niles.

For we omitted to mention, in its appropriate connection, that when Molly found herself laid under the responsibility of naming her boy, she was debarred from bestowing on him that of his father, since it had been previously appropriated among the six, and her artistic sense revolted from starting the poor, helpless innocent out in the world under the honored designation of Zophar Tupper, which his grandfather had borne with such eminent respectability. And so, being influenced by the tender grace of motherhood, and desirous of showing her kind feeling towards the man whom she had once so loved and had now so freely forgiven, she felt that she could do it in no more expressive way than by calling her baby John Avery. The compliment was appreciated, and there may still be seen, among the family treasures of the Niles tribe, a silver cup, of punchy form and curious workmanship, marked with the inscription "J. A. N. from J. A."

Jack the second grew up a tolerably correct copy of the boyhood of his namesake. He was gifted with the same gayety of temperament, and facility for getting into scrapes. It had happened more than once that heedless pranks of his had been leniently looked upon, and concealed or remedied by the considerate care of John the elder, who, spite of all the miserable warping and drying up of all his kindlier sympathies under the influence of that ever-impending possibility, still seemed to find a congenial satisfaction in the society of this frank, jolly youth, whose presence brought with it such an echo of his own once careless, joyous life.

But, spite of warnings and admonitions, Jack was still a sad boy, and his favorite mode of working off his surplus activity was in devising and executing practical jokes. His invention and audacity reached their culmination in a most unprincipled scheme against the two venerable Avery cousins.

Philo was now as sour, dry, and wizened an old man as dwelt in the state of Connecticut, and those bleak hills and stony slopes do not seem to produce very ripe and mellow old age. But Philo was known as an especially hard and grasping old sinner, living a sort of dog's life, all by himself, and too stingy to open his eyes wide. And it befell once that he and his strange, barren mode of life were touched upon in the evening talk of the Niles family, and then the mother, with her old, modest sprightliness, went over the story of the two wills made so long ago, and which must, in the natural course of human events, soon come into effect. She had grown to be an old woman, this blessed mother, but none of the loving ones, to whom her presence had been a joy and consolation for so many years, ever thought of her gray hairs or caps or spectacles, except as the emblems of more abundant peace and benediction.

She tells her story now, — about the early days of the two old men, whose withered faces, and bent forms, and eager, acquisitive eyes are so familiar to them all, — and as she proceeds, Jack lapses from lively attention to a mood of profound reflection, which is always a bad sign for somebody.

In the evening twilight of the next day, a thin, yellow-haired lad, mounted on a large, bony, sorrel horse, presented himself with an appearance of great haste and urgency before the door of Philo Avery's hermetic dwelling. After a vigorous though fruitless knocking, he made his way to the rear of the small, dismal brown house, and spied an aged figure advancing from an adjacent piece of woods, bending under the weight of a large heap of brush.

"Be you Philo Avery?"

"Yes," answered the ancient, with evident suspicion.

"Then I've got a letter for you," said the thin youth, and, thrusting it forth, sprang upon his high horse and clattered away down the road.

A letter! Philo stood and watched the messenger till he disappeared from sight, filled with a vague sense that something strange was about to break upon him. A letter sent to him was in itself a strange occurrence. Who could write to him? and for what? Could it indeed be the one thing so long looked for? and, if it were, how sudden! Tremulous with excitement, he trotted into the house, and, after many minutes of agitated fumbling, succeeded in lighting a candle. Then he held the letter close and tried to examine the address, for Philo was a victim to that unaccountable oddity, to which the greater portion of human nature is prone, of making a close and critical scrutiny of any unexpected or mysterious letter, before opening it for the conclusive knowledge of its contents. But everything looks misty before his eyes, and, after much squinting and peering, it occurs to him that he has forgotten his spectacles. And at last, after more delay and fumbling, he comes to the subject matter, very brief but comprehensive: —

"John Avery died last night. Funeral at ten o'clock to-morrow morning."

No date, no signature; but what of that? Over and over Philo read the two lines, before his mind could really grasp the intelligence they conveyed. It would have made a striking picture, — that withered, bent figure, in its coarse, well-worn clothes, stooping in the dim, lonely room, and the hungry eyes devouring that bit of news. It had happened at last, this thing for which he has waited almost half a century. How many hundred times he had imagined his own feelings when it should come to him, and how different it all was! The old man sinks into a chair and gives himself up to revery. And sitting thus, there come stealing upon him remembrances of long past scenes. He thinks of the time when he and John were boys together, and of all his mother's love and care of both; of the parting on the deck of the Skylark, and their long voyage. And then came the slow-moving panorama of all the dull, dreary, barren years that dragged their slow length onward between his present self and all these boyish memories. The hours pass unnoted as the poor old man goes through the successive stages of his retrospect, and finally arouses himself with a start when the candle, that has been burning dim and flickering, gives a dying glare and goes out in the socket. And then he arises, cramped and stiff, and creeps trembling to bed as the cocks are crowing for midnight. But the newly-made heir cannot sleep. Haunting images visit him, as the Furies surrounded Orestes. At length he rises and seeks the repository of his valuables. He takes out the will, and though he has known it, every word by heart, for a whole generation's lifetime, he reads it mechanically over. How strange the lines look, and the name of *Zophar Tupper*, written with the old magisterial flourish! Here, too, are the signatures of the witnesses, and he finds himself wondering why John never married Molly after all, and, even now, does not dream that he himself was the obstacle, by his disagreeable persistency in living; for our mortality is the last and severest lesson that we learn in life.

Philo wonders if it is not almost daylight, and looks out at the east window for the first streak of dawn; reflects that he must start early, for it is nine miles to the town, and his old horse is not over-active. He will have to dress up, too, for the funeral. How strange! To pass away the time, he begins to get out his clothes and lay them ready. From the depths of a great red chest he brings up a pair of good, new pantaloons, that he has not worn for ten years, and then a coat to match, and a fine shirt with a ruffled bosom, that Aunt Betsy made for him while she was still young enough to do such things. And, lastly, he bethinks himself of a pair of black linen gloves that he bought on the occasion of the good woman's funeral, and from the darkest corner of the chest he fishes them up. A little dingy and rotten they are, to be sure, but still in wonderful preservation, though they give way in two or three spots when he puts them carefully on.

In these little occupations he wears away the hours till the darkness begins to grow gray, and as soon as he can see sufficiently he goes to the pasture and leads his astonished old horse to the door. Then comes the terrible process of shaving; — and what spectacle is more forlorn than that of an old bachelor trying to shave a long, stiff beard by a weak light and with cold water? Even this is at length achieved; and then, after much brushing and other unaccustomed elaborations of toilet, he places the will carefully in his pocket, and, drawing on the rusty gloves, takes a final survey of himself before starting. The mouldy little mirror reflects a thin, yellow face dried into long, fine wrinkles, straggling gray locks, and watery, pale-blue eyes. The old-fashioned clothes make the thin, stooping figure more awkward and spindling, and a high, tight cravat completes the scarecrow effect of the whole. Still Philo has done his best, and is satisfied, as he mounts his ancient steed, that he presents the very likeness of respectable sorrow.

And jogging decorously onward, as becomes his dismal errand, he ponders how different this morning is from all the other mornings of his life. In the silver-gray dawn there come back all the strange sentiments that had arisen out of the surprise and excitement of the previous midnight. A thick mist creeps up from a little stream that runs by the road-side, and its damp, clinging chill seems to strike through and saturate his very vitals. It occurs to him that the road is very lonely, and the few scattered farm-houses very dreary and inhospitable-looking, for it is a cloudy morning, and people are not yet stirring.

All the influences and associations of the hour are dreary and funereal. He tries to fix his mind upon the inheritance into which he is about to step, but no bright, alluring visions rise at his call, and his thoughts are either perpetually recurring to the early memories that so affected him the night before, or else to the suggestion of his own form lying stiff and cold for burial in the place of his cousin's. All the well-known landmarks of the familiar way start into new and strange aspects; and he recoils in affright from an old guideboard that has stood in exactly the same place for forty years, but now appears like some spectral gallows that spreads its arms in ghostly invitation. He twists and pinches himself as he rides along, to be assured that he is in the world of realities; but the night's experiences have unstrung his aged nerves, and mind and body quiver helplessly alike.

And now, from the brow of a little eminence, he perceives a gig slowly advancing from below, and, as it nears him, he becomes conscious of a great familiarity in its appearance. It is certainly very like the one that John bought so long ago, before Molly was married, and which he has used ever since. Curiously, too, it is drawn by a white horse, and John has had a white horse for ages past. This is indeed a coincidence. The thing comes noiselessly nearer. Oh, horror of horrors! It is John's own self, — his form, — his features, — his old brown hat, — John indeed, but deadly pale, and with wide, wild eyes fixed in a terrible stony gaze. No natural look, no nod of recognition, but only that hideous, glassy stare as he comes silently along, riding up out of the white fog.

Philo can neither move nor cry out. He would turn and escape, but his stiffened hand refuses to draw the rein, and his horse has become, like himself, rigid and motionless.

Prayers, oaths, and invocations rush, in a confused huddle, through his bewildered brain, as he sits and gazes, unable to remove his eyes from that horrid sight, and while he is vainly seeking to frame his lips to some sort of utterance, the wraith itself breaks the silence.

"Philo." The tone is broken and distant.

Trembling and choked, he tries to answer. The blood

rushes to his face and almost blinds him, and he stammers out, —

"John Avery, — aren't you dead?"

"Are you?" asks the wraith.

"I — I — I don't know," says Philo, and he didn't.

The ghost rises, steps down from the gig, and extends his hand. It is very cold and clammy, but still a sound, fleshly hand, though quite hard and shrunken from its early proportions.

"Thank God!" shouts Philo Avery.

"*Thank God!*" responds John Avery, fervently.

"How came you here?" asks Philo, still a little incredulous as to the real mortality of his companion.

"On my way to attend your funeral," says John.

"Why, no, — that can't be, — I'm going to yours."

"Heavens!" exclaims John.

"I guess it's a hoax," suggests Philo.

John takes out a letter and reads aloud: "*Philo Avery died last night. Funeral at ten o'clock to-morrow morning.*"

"Just like mine, except the name," says Philo. "So you thought I was a ghost."

"Didn't know what else you could be. You looked queer enough for one," replied John.

"Well, I've lived long enough to see ghosts, but this is the first of that kind of gentry that ever showed themselves to me," cried Philo, in his high, cracked voice, and actually convulsed with laughter. John joined in, and the two ghosts made the whole region alive.

"It must have been somebody that knew about the wills," said John, when they had grown calm.

"Yes," replied Philo; "and what cursed things they have been?"

"Cursed — for both of us," said John.

"Have you got it along with you?"

"Yes, of course, — have you?" answered John, reddening faintly.

"Why, yes, — and here it goes," cried Philo, with sudden energy, pulling it out, and shredding it in strips. John was not to be outdone. With equal eagerness he pulled his out, and, in a few seconds, both the wills were fluttering in fragments among the elderberry bushes by the road-side.

"What a contemptible old screw I've been!" exclaimed John, penitentially, as the insurance table came into his mind.

"No worse than I," said Philo, thinking of all his drudging, grovelling years.

"Why, do you know I've wished you dead," burst out John.

"Well, suppose you have, — I've done the same by you," answered Philo.

"May God forgive us both."

"*Amen*," said Philo, solemnly.

"And help us in the future," continued John.

"Amen again," said Philo.

The muffled clatter of a horse's hoofs sounded through the fog, and presently the twinkling face of Jack Niles beamed upon the ghostly couple. Looking with well simulated astonishment on the group, the empty gig, and his venerable namesake standing in the middle of the road, Jack paused and begged to know what was the trouble, and whether he could be of service.

"I believe it was you," said Philo, looking at the mischievous lad with sudden prescience.

"I know 'twas," said John.

And though Jack never owned it, that was a conviction that never departed from the minds of the two, and when they died, long after, he found himself bound by substantial reasons to remember the Two Ghosts of New London Turnpike.

DOWN BY THE SEA.

Down by the Sea.

THERE is a lonely old house situated close down by the sea, in one of the most secluded yet lonely nooks, not far from one of the most noted resorts on the seaboard; an old gray stone house, showing the marks of the many wild storms which have beat upon it in all the long years which have passed over it; a house whose bareness and desolation are enlivened but little by the heavy-trailing ivy which creeps over a portion of it and in which many wild birds build their nests. Old as it is, it seems never to have been finished,—rather to have been left without any of the last touches which complete a building, and to have thus stood for many years, with the wild winds and storms of the coast beating against it. Here and there a shutter is torn from its hinges, and lies where it fell under the window. The point is entirely gone from cornice and colonnade, and the floor of the latter, which had never been painted, is old and worm-eaten. The grounds about it are an intricate tangle of brushwood. Flowering shrubs, which had been planted here and there, have grown up into wild and unshapely trees. Rose-bushes and wild vines choke up the paths, and the gates and fences are broken and dilapidated. There is one path, which leads down to the beach, which has been kept open, and has, apparently, been often trodden; but apart from this there seems to be but little sign of life around the old gray house. There is, indeed, one red-curtained window upon the side which looks out to sea, and here a bright light is always burning at night, and all night, and the sailors have learned to watch for it as for a signal; and the place is known to them as the Lone-Star House. Let us watch around the house, and perhaps it will have a story to tell, — such places often do have, lonely and deserted as they seem; stories often full enough of human love and heart-break. "It looks as though it might be haunted," say the gay parties who ride by it from the fashionable resort a few miles away. Yes, and there is no doubt but what it is.

"All houses wherein men have lived and died
Are haunted houses. Through the open doors
Phantoms unseen upon their errands glide
With feet that make no noise upon the floors."

It is growing sunset now, and the sky is blossoming most gloriously with many-colored clouds, as out of the door of the old house a woman glides and takes the beaten path to the beach. A great rough and shaggy dog follows her, and the two together walk thoughtfully along. They go down where the great waves are tumbling and tossing upon the rocks, and pace rapidly up and down the shore, looking far out over the green waters with their fleecy crowns of foam. She is a woman of middle-age, verging near upon forty, one would say, tall, and straight as an arrow, with large, unfathomable gray eyes and a massive coronal of glossy hair, streaked here and there with gray. She wears a cheap, dark dress; but she has a handsome scarlet shawl around her shoulders, of the most superb tint of which you can conceive; and she looks like a woman who would love rich and gorgeous coloring; and, indeed, it is one of her passions. In draperies, in articles of dress where such colors are admissible, and more than all in flowers and leaves, she loves the deepest and richest tints. Every night the sunset is a revelation to her. She studies the gorgeous castles and cathedrals of gold, which are builded in the western heavens with a glory which the temple of Solomon could never attain; and she watches, from her little turret window up in the old gray house yonder, every morning for the rising of the great high-priest in his garments resplendent. There was, indeed, something warm and rich and tropical in her blood, albeit it sprung from the cold New England fount. She reminded one, as much as anything, of

"The wondrous valley hidden in the depths of Gloucester woods
Full of plants which love the summer blooms of warmer latitudes,
Where the Arctic birch is broided by the tropic's flowery vines,
And the silver-starred magnolia lights the twilight of the pines."

She walks upon the beach till the sunset has burned low in the red west, and then takes the path back to the house. When about half-way across the garden, she turns off a little from the main path, and, putting back the bushes with her hands, makes her way for a few paces and stops at a little grave, — a child's grave, — tufted thick with purple pansies, sprinkled with white daisies. She sits down for a moment beside it, plucks one or two spires of grass which have sprung up among the flowers, then hurriedly leaves it, calling her dog after her, and going into the house, where the light soon shines in the seaward-looking window. The woman's name is Agnes Wayland, and here she has lived alone for now nearly twenty years, — alone, except once in a while of a summer she takes a quiet boarder or two, who see little of her and know less, and of whom she esteems it a great pleasure to be well rid, when the autumnal equinox comes on. Winter and summer, in storm and sleet, rain and shine, she stays shut in the dim old house all day, and emerges only towards evening for her walk upon the beach, and her peep at the little grave, with its coverlet of pansies in summer and its white drapery of snow in winter. Upon the night of which I have been writing, she made her way back, as I have said, into her own room, — a room where her prevailing tastes could quickly be discovered. A peculiar depth and brilliancy of coloring pervaded everything; carpet and curtains were of the same vivid crimson, and the large bay-window filled with plants was gorgeous as a festal-room of the fairies. Everything was old and much worn, and had a look of old but not faded splendor. A few books occupied a cabinet in one corner, and a piano, which was always locked, stood in another. An easy-chair was drawn up to a little stand, near the window, and upon it lay an open Bible. This was the place where she sat and read hour by hour and day by day, always from the Bible, only varying her occupation by weary hours over intricate and elaborate pieces of fancy-work, — more beautiful and marvellous than such pieces of work ever were made before, but always things which required only mechanical kind of ingenuity, and needed genius and taste only in the coloring, — and these she sold at the nearest town, and so earned her daily bread. After she had taken her accustomed seat this evening, she was startled by a ring at the door, — a sound so unusual that she trembled like a leaf as she took the lamp and started to answer the summons. She had got half-way down the stairs, when she stopped, and called lightly to the dog, who was beside her in a moment, and together they opened the door. A grave-looking elderly gentleman stood there, who inquired if he had the honor of addressing Mrs. Wayland.

"That is my name, sir," she answered, not opening the door or bidding him enter.

"And mine is Ashly, madam. I am a clergyman, living in Boston, and I am seeking a quiet place, near the sea, in which to spend the summer. I have been told in the village yonder that you sometimes receive a boarder, and I think your place will just suit me. I have recommendations, if you wish."

But Mrs. Wayland did not need them. She was too good a judge of character, despite her long seclusion, not to see at a glance that he was what he asserted, and that, if she must have boarders at all, he was just what she wanted. So she invited him in, without relaxing a particle in the coldness of her demeanor, and, giving him a seat in a cheerless-looking and scantily-furnished dining-room, told him in as few words as possible what she would do for him and for how much she would do it, — a straightforwardness which raised her very highly in the reverend doctor's estimation, although she designed, if she had a design in the matter, quite a contrary effect. She had sometimes had some trouble in keeping her boarders at a sufficient distance to suit her, and she had found it necessary upon their first arrival to have it distinctly understood that they were to expect no sort of companionship from her; that she gave them a room and their board, such as it was, and she never took any pains to make it good or attractive, and that that was all she wanted of them. But Dr. Ashly had a great horror of a bustling and gossipy landlady, and thought he had found a perfect treasure; and when she had shown him the room he could have, if he liked, he eagerly agreed to take it, and said if she had no objection he would take possession forthwith, and not go back to the village till morning. To this she assented indifferently, and soon left him alone, calling the one house-maid to get him some supper, and, retiring to her own room, was soon buried in her accustomed thoughts, and scarcely aware of his existence. And as landlady and lodger were equally pleased to let each other alone, there was little intercourse between them for several weeks. But one night, when the doctor had been for a long walk on the beach, he saw, as he was returning, Mrs. Wayland, in her usual evening exercise, pacing up and down the beach, and was struck by her appearance as she walked thus, and stood still for a time observing her, and followed her at last, at a little distance, while she made her visit to the child's grave. His kind heart was very much touched by the sight, and he determined to talk with her and give her his sympathy and friendship, if she needed them. So he gathered some of the pansies off from the grave, and, holding them in his hand, went into tea. Mrs. Wayland had laid aside her shawl and was already seated at the table. They usually had little conversation at these times, and that of the most commonplace character. This evening, as he came through the door and she caught sight of the flowers in his hand, she exclaimed, in a quick, excited way, "You have been to my grave!"

She spoke as though he had intruded upon her most sacred privacy, and he answered, apologetically, "Yes, I have visited the little grave in the garden. I hope I have not intruded. I have a little grave in the churchyard at home, and such spots are very sacred to me."

Agnes Wayland was a lady, and she would not have

been guilty of a rudeness for the world, so she hastened to reply, —

"Oh, no, sir, you have not been guilty of intrusion, but you are the first one who has ever visited my grave, and I have watched it so fondly for so many years that I almost felt jealous that any other eyes should ever look upon it."

"And I have not only looked upon it," said the minister, very softly and benignantly, "but I have dropped a tear upon it."

"That is something that I have never done."

"Then I pity you with all my heart, my friend. If I had not been able to weep over my child's grave, I think my heart would have broken."

"Mine, sir, was broken before the child died," and, as she said this, she arose hastily and left the room.

The minister was much interested and full of sympathy for this lonely woman, whose lot was so isolated, and as he lay that night and listened to the deep, hollow roar of the sea, he thought of the great deeps of the human heart, and the fierce passions which were ever tossing it, and of the great calm of death.

A few days after he ventured as delicately as he could to return to the subject, by referring to the little girl he had lost, and of how her mother had followed her, but a short time before, to the better land.

"You seem very cheerful, sir," said Agnes Wayland, in a quick, impetuous way, "and yet you have had trouble, it seems."

"Yes, madam, I have had some very severe and dreadful trials; but I am very happy and hopeful in spite of them all, for I know that now they will soon be ended, and that I shall recover all that I have lost when I reach the heavenly land."

"How do you know that? I don't know it. When I buried my only child down in the garden there, I thought I had lost him forever. That was why, in my stony grief, no tear ever fell upon his grave. I have been trying these fifteen years to believe what you say you believe; but it has no consolation for me. God took my child away from me in my bitterest need, and he took him forever. Was it a good God who did that?"

Her voice was cold and rigid, and a pallor as of death was upon her face as she paused for a reply.

"A good God, madam! and whom he loveth he chasteneth!"

"No, indeed, sir, I don't believe that. He didn't love me, and I didn't love him, and I don't love him now, — hate him, rather. He has tried me too sorely."

"My dear friend, you know not what you say. I beseech you, do not blaspheme your God."

"I have only said, sir, for once, what I have been thinking all these dreadful years. When I buried my child down there, I did not believe in any God for years. I thought some vile and fiendish Fate was pursuing me. Then you ministers were always saying to me, 'Pray;' and I prayed. They said to me, 'Study the word of God;' and I studied it. It has been my only study for fifteen years, and it has brought me no consolation yet."

"But you have found God in it, — have you not? You do not deny a God?"

"I have found a God in it certainly, but only a God who has separated me eternally from all I love."

"My dear friend, I assure you, you have not yet found the true God, if you believe this."

"I have found I verily believe the God of the Bible, and he has said the wicked shall go away into everlasting punishment; and I am the most wicked of all God's creatures."

Here Mrs. Wayland left him again standing upon the colonnade, and hurried rapidly from him down the path which led to the sea. Her conversation had revived in her heart all the strong passions which slumbered there, and which she usually held in close repression. As she paced wildly up and down the beach, feeling in her nearness to the sea a sort of comfort as though the great ocean were her friend, she thought over her whole lonely life. She thought of her happy and brilliant youth, of its gayeties, its triumphs, and its great hopes; she beheld herself the petted darling of a joyous circle of companions and friends. She thought of her journeys in distant lands, whither a loving father had taken her, and of all the delights of those years when they had wandered through all the sunny climes of southern Europe, and so away on to the Orient, where she had trodden with pilgrim feet all the sacred places of that

Holy Land. It was there she had first met her husband; and she dwelt with fondness upon every little incident which memory recalled of her intercourse with him there, and of how they had sailed together upon their return to their native land. It was then she had learned to love the ocean. In those long days, when they were out upon the trackless deep, they had learned together the sweet mystery of loving. Night after night they had paced the deck together, gazing out upon the moonlighted expanse, and watching the breakers rise and fall. The long voyage had been a season of enchantment. It had passed into her being, and become a part of her inmost life forever. She had one of those natures to whom such things come but once in a lifetime. When they had reached home, they had been married, and, after a year or two of pleasant married life, they had built the old gray house of which I have told you, designing to pass their summers down there within hearing of the grand, eternal anthem of the sea. How well she remembered the hurry they were in to get down here,— so great a hurry that they could not stop to have the house entirely finished, and so in early May they had furnished two or three rooms, and lived there in a wild trance of what seems to her now, as she looks back upon it, perfect bliss. Here they wandered up and down the beach together hand in hand for hours and beheld the waters glowing in the early tints of sunrise, and reflecting the gorgeous splendors of sunset, and rippling and shimmering in the bewildering moonlight.

Then she thinks of how gayeties began up at the village yonder, and how they began to see much company and to mingle in all the excitements of watering-place life. Here they had met the beautiful syren who had stolen her husband from her. With what angry hate she dwells upon the soft, bewildering beauty of that woman, — her rounded, dimpled form, her golden hair, and the languishing blueness of the dreamy eyes! She seemed in all her bewitching beauty, to the eye of Agnes Wayland, more hateful and hideous than a fiend. She had fascinated Mortimer Wayland almost from their first meeting. Of a dreamy, sensuous temperament, and a weak will, and with no great power of principle at his back, the artful and wicked woman had ensnared him with her wiles, and in the meshes of her charms he had forgotten the grand and queenly wife, who to every eye was so infinitely the superior of one for whom he was deserting her, and the little year-old baby, who was just learning to lisp "father" to him as he fondled him.

Of the wild tempest which tossed her soul at this time she dreaded to think even now. It had been so near to madness that it was a terror to her yet. But pride had always been one of her ruling passions, and, instead of pleading with him with a woman's tenderness, as some might have done, she had treated him with coldness and disdain, and with reproachful scorn had goaded him on to take the last step in the dreadful drama.

He had deserted her, and with the blue-eyed woman had sailed for a distant land. Never since that time, now nearly twenty years, had she left, except for her lonely walks, the old gray house. She shut herself up like a hermit, and with wild and bitter grief cursed herself and her God. Down into the deepest gloom of despair she went, where never a single ray of heavenly light and comfort reached her. Her child, indeed, she had left; but although she loved him with all the concentrated passion of her nature, he seemed little comfort to her. She brooded continually upon the darkness of her fate, and upon the fathomless depths of despair into which she was sinking.

Then the child died, and her last human interest went; and she made its little grave in the tangled garden, and every year covered it thick with flowers. But in her heart no white blossom of hope had ever sprung up, no purple pansy of royal magnanimity and forgiveness had yet blossomed there. And this night, after so many years, she was living it all over again with tragic interest, and no softened feelings of relenting or forgiveness entered her stern heart.

"He is very happy," she thought to herself as she wended her way back and stood by her little grave; "he is very happy, for he can stand by his child's bed and weep; and so could I, if I had his hope. O my darling, my darling, darling boy!" and she stooped down, and threw her arms caressingly over the little mound.

"Oh, if God would only, only let me meet you once more! O my God, why cannot I forgive and be forgiven?"

"My sister," said the kind old man, coming up and hearing her last words; and feeling how vain it would be to reason or expostulate with this woman, — "let us pray;" and, almost before she knew it, they were kneeling by the little one's grave; and before the old minister had concluded his simple but touching prayer, the woman, whose heart had been stone for so many years, was weeping, weeping with passionate sobs like a little child; and when he had concluded, she arose, and without a word made her way into the house, and soon the red light shone in the little window.

Somehow after this a more gentle feeling crept into the heart of Mrs. Wayland. A softer light came into her eye, and a more gentle tremor was in her voice as she addressed the old minister, who saw that she was touched, but was too wise to meddle farther than was absolutely necessary with the good work which he was sure was going on.

It was not many weeks from the evening of which I have spoken, when, as she was returning from her evening walk, she beheld a scene of bustle around the door of her house; a carriage was driving away, and a trunk stood upon the steps, while some figures seemed just entering the door whom she could not distinguish in the gathering darkness. "Dr. Ashly has some friends come," she thought, with a feeling of impatience; "what shall I do with them?" and she walked quickly to the house. As she turned into the cheerless dining-room, — the only room which was ever used below, — she saw, stretched upon a couch, the figure of a man propped up by pillows, which seemed to have been hastily brought, and looking pallid and wan. She walked quickly forward, but when she had reached the middle of the room, she stopped like one transfixed, and, with wild eyes full of eagerness and something like joy, looked about her.

"Mortimer Wayland!" she exclaimed at last, grasping the table for support. "Why come you here?"

"I have come home to die, Agnes. I could not die anywhere else; I have been for years trying to do so, — but God would not let me. I was forced to come and seek your forgiveness, and God will not take me until I have it; yet I dare not ask you to grant it; it is too much!" At this the sick man shut his eyes wearily, and said no more.

"Forgive us our sins as we forgive those who trespass against us," solemnly said the voice of the old minister, who was sitting near the couch upon which the man lay.

"Oh, sir, you cannot know what it is for me to ask of her. Most wrongs may be forgiven; but mine against her is so great that she cannot forgive me, I am sure, unless God helps her. I have been suffering for it these twenty years, — trying to expiate it; but I have failed. I have suffered, I have struggled, I have almost died many times, sir; but I could not atone for my sin, and God could not forgive it, nor can she."

Then the minister's voice was heard again, and it said, "Sister, remember the little child's grave in the garden, and forgive and be forgiven."

Then Mrs. Wayland, who had stood like a statue all this time, rushed forward, and, kneeling by the couch poured forth her whole heart in a torrent of passionate words, —

"O my husband, my darling, my only love, forgive me for my coldness and my scorn! forgive me for not helping you to withstand temptation, — I, who was always the stronger! It was I who drove you away, and for it I have suffered and agonized all these years. I have been so hard, so wicked and cruel, so unpitying and unforgiving, that I have had no rest or peace night or day. It is so blessed to feel that I forgive you! so joyful to think that you will forgive me, — that God will forgive us both!" and the woman laid her head upon his breast, and rained upon his lips a thousand passionate kisses.

Then Dr. Ashly would have left them; but the woman called him back.

"Share in our great joy, dear friend," she said; "for, had it not been for you, this would never have been. A few weeks ago I should never have received him whom I loved even as I had always loved, but whom my pride would have banished from my door in the face of all his pleadings; but you have softened my heart, and to you we owe this joyful hour. And now you must help me," she continued, with a woman's thoughtful care, "to carry him to my own room upstairs, which is the only comfortable room I have; and there I can nurse him up, and soon have him well again."

And so he was carried up to the room where she had sat alone so many years, and was soon as comfortable as womanly care could make him.

"How natural it all looks here!" he said, glancing around the room. "It is just as it used to be,—isn't it, darling? And I remember it so well,—furnished, to suit you, in crimson, which you still like, as I see by your shawl."

"Yes," she said, with a little blush; "I have always worn it for your sake. You used to say it was just the color to suit me, and I have worn it all these years."

"Darling," said he, looking all about the room, "I see no traces of any one but yourself here. Where is our child,—our little baby boy?"

Agnes Wayland went softly up to him, and put her arms around his neck, as she said,—

"I thought, a few weeks ago, that he was down in the garden under a bed of pansies; but now I know he is in heaven, where you and I will soon join him."

WHY MRS. RADNOR FAINTED.

WHY MRS. RADNOR FAINTED.

YOU have seen hazel eyes,—have you not? I don't mean the quiet nut-brown ones, you meet every day, but *bona fide* hazel eyes, opaline in their wonderful changes,—that make you wonder, when you turn away from them, what color they will have assumed when you next look into their depths; for such eyes have depths, sometimes glowing emerald-like, with a steady, lambent flame, now gleaming with a soft lustre like pearls, or melted into sapphires by tears.

Such eyes had Mrs. Radnor,—cold, beautiful woman that she was; insensible, I was about to say, only I remember her fainting at sight of a pond-lily. How well I recollect the day! There was a party of us passing the midsummer at the old Richmond farm, a few miles from ——; Mr. and Mrs. Ferdinand Radnor among the rest. The latter, a haughty statuesque woman, with nothing save her wonderful eyes to indicate anything approaching a heart,—lovely as a dream, yet with beauty that repelled even in its fascination. Such hair, too, as she had, rolling in golden ripples down to her slender feet; — fine as silk, it was brown in the shade, but glowed and intensified in the light till it seemed as if a thousand stray sunbeams were imprisoned in the radiant mass. We always called her the "Princess with the golden locks." You remember her in the fairy tale, — do you not? That one, I mean, whose hair was the wonder and admiration of the whole world, and whose lovers delighted to bind themselves with fetters so exquisite; yet when they strove playfully to throw them off, they found themselves with gyves and manacles of steel, under which they were powerless.

Mr. Radnor was urbane and gentlemanly; but, possessing only half a soul, he divided the interest of that equally between admiring his own person and annoying Mrs. Radnor by his attentions.

It was a sultry July day, and we were all of us on the rose-terrace back of the house, some dozing, — I pretending to read, though all the time watching the "Princess" furtively from the shelter of my book.

She had a pile of cushions spread with a scarlet shawl, and, like an Eastern beauty, lay languidly upon them. Her dress of palest blue was open at the throat, and her hands toyed listlessly with the heavy cord that confined her waist. There was a blush-rose tint on her usually pale cheek, and her hair, half escaped from its little net, lay like flecks of gold on the scarlet cover. I think I never saw repose, utter and perfect, before.

"Down through her limbs a drooping languor crept,
Her head a little bent, and on her mouth
A doubtful smile dwelt like a clouded moon
In a still water."

Suddenly the charmed silence was broken, for round the corner of the house came Mr. Radnor, with his arms filled with superb water-lilies, which he threw in a fragrant shower over his wife. He was saluted with exclamations of wonder and delight, and while he was replying, I had leisure to observe his wife.

The change was frightful: an ashen pallor had spread itself over her face, she was panting violently for breath, and, at the same time, attempting to clasp both hands before her eyes. I cried aloud and sprang towards her, — but it was too late.

Mrs. Radnor had fainted!

At the same time, Anne Richmond threw herself upon her knees beside her, and, hastily gathering the snowy flowers from her dress and bosom, where they had fallen, thrust them into Mr. Radnor's arms, saying hurriedly, as she did so, —

"Pray, pray, take them away, sir, or your wife will die."

He obeyed blankly, and together Anne and I applied the usual restoratives, and, after some minutes, were rewarded by a faint color in her lips, then a quivering of the mouth, and I heard her murmur faintly, — "I saw him again, Anne. Oh, those dreadful flowers!"

Then her eyes opened, — those wonderful eyes, that were then almost startling in their blackness. She looked wildly round her for a single second, and, catching sight of me, was herself again, — haughty, self-sustained as before, even though lying helpless as a child on Anne Richmond's arms.

And, after all, pride is better for a fainting woman than all the sal volatile in the world, thought I, receiving her languidly uttered thanks, and retreating.

We saw no more of Mrs. Radnor that day. Her husband talked loudly of the extreme heat; and no one but the two who had observed the expression of her face when the perfume of the lilies first met her senses, knew anything to the contrary. As for me, I was restless and unquiet. There had been from the first a nameless something about Mrs. Radnor which had excited my deepest interest, and now my imagination was busy. One thing the painful scene of the morning had convinced me of, and that was, that some time in the past she had been quickened into life by the breath of love, and the flowers had played a terrible part in overwhelming her with memories possibly long buried in the deepest recesses of her heart; for — I acknowledged it — Mrs. Radnor had a heart. I never doubted it from the moment in which her face changed from its quiet repose into that torturing expression of fear that it wore when she fainted.

" Anne," I said that evening to Miss Richmond, as I drew her into my chamber after the party had separated for the night, " tell me something of Mrs. Radnor. I am sure you are in some way concerned in her past."

"Yes," she answered, with a little, fluttering sigh; "there is one page of her life that no one living has ever read but myself. Perhaps I do wrong in consenting to turn it for you; but it may be a warning to you, child. To-morrow we will go down to the lake together, and I will tell you what has changed Mrs. Radnor, from the brightest, sunniest girl that ever lived, to the breathing statue that she has been for ten years."

She sighed again, as she kissed my cheek, and then I heard her footsteps die away in the long corridor.

My room was in the second story, and directly over those occupied by the Radnors, which opened on a balcony leading down by a little flight of steps to the lawn.

The night was sultry and still. All the usual bustle and stir of retiring had ceased, and, extinguishing my candle, I curled myself on the broad window-seat, watching the stars that seemed to smile in the hazy atmosphere. It was late,—nearly midnight, I think; and I drank with delight the heavy fragrance which that hour always seems to draw from the heliotrope, great masses of which grew under my windows. I do not know how long I sat there. Waking dreams, such as flit lightly in the tender stillness of summer nights, wooed me with delicious repose. I fancied myself beneath Eastern skies, and the faint stir of a bird in a neighboring tree seemed to me the pluming of a bulbul's wing; and through the gilded lattice of the harem two starry eyes—and they were Mrs. Radnor's—glittered and gleamed. The soft running of a brook through the grounds was the lapping of waves against Venice stones. I heard the twinkle of a guitar, and, framed by carved, gray stone work, her rippling golden hair stirred in the night-breeze.

Then everything faded, and I slept a moment or an hour, — I cannot say which, so softly had the hours passed in softest sandals, — and it was with a start that I sat upright and heard, with a keen thrill of fear, a faint click, as of a drawn bolt, and immediately the distant bell of St. Michael's pealing out.

One — two; and with the dying of the second stroke there was a rustling sound beneath my window, and then a shuddering whisper, — "My God! my God! have mercy upon me!"

Shrouded by a half-closed blind, I peered out, and, kneeling on the balcony below, I saw a white figure illuminated by the strange, weird light of a waning moon. The face was uplifted, and the expression might have been that worn by Maria Therese in the solitude of her chamber when the Archduchess Josepha died.

I drew back, — it seemed like profanity for any but the God to whom she appealed to witness her despair, — for it was Mrs. Radnor. I heard a long, deep-drawn sigh, a footstep, and then the silky tones of her husband.

"My love, — why will you? The dew is very heavy." Then a stir and the sound of a closing door.

I shivered in the ghostly light that had crept into my window, and, softly closing my blinds, I laid down to sleep if I could.

The first person I saw, on entering the breakfast-room the next morning, was Mrs. Radnor, pale as the muslin wrapper she wore, but as coldly self-contained as usual. I felt the passionate sympathy, which had taken firm hold on me since the scenes of the previous night, almost vanish before her languidly uttered replies to my inquiries for her health. It was only in watching the drooping corners of her rarely beautiful mouth and the violet circles beneath the wonderful eyes, that I could connect the haughty being before me with the utterer of the despairing cry of the night before.

The day wore on slowly enough to me, and it was only when the lengthened shadows on the terrace, and Miss Richmond, equipped for her walk, greeted my eyes, that my impatience subsided.

The path led us through a shady grove of pines, that sighed mournfully as one passed through them, then across a sloping interval made green by recent rains, and so down through a fringe of alders to a little seat close by the margin of a charming lake on which myriads of water-lilies were closing their cups of incense.

"Sit here," said Anne, pointing to a place at her side.

"It is not always pleasant to think or speak of the past," she began, after a few moments' silence, "although day by day its scenes and actors appear to us. There are some memories in every heart that thrill us with grief unutterable, and when you know that one person in the story which I shall tell you was dear to me as my own soul, you will not wonder if my lip falters or I fail to dwell on the more painful portions of it."

Then for the first time I was aware of another unwritten heart-history, and knew why the soft lips and eyes of the woman beside me had so often uttered their fatal no.

"Ten years ago," she said, "our house was full of guests, and among them was Eleanor Orne, — the most perfectly beautiful girl I ever beheld. Fancy Mrs. Radnor, younger by as many years, with a bewildering smile ever ready to play around the lovely mouth, with expressions as rapidly following themselves in her eyes as clouds on an April day, and you can form a faint idea of her loveliness.

"There was also a young student of divinity, with an eye as clear as a star and a soul pure as prayer itself. Proud and calm he was; but it was a noble pride that clothed him as with a garment, and a gracious calmness resulting from a vaulting intellect, subdued and chastened by firmest faith.

"He had been fond of me in a way, but from the night that Eleanor came floating down the long piazza, attired in some diaphanous gray that streamed around her like mist, I knew how it would be. I marked, with one great heart-throb, the perfect delight that flashed in his dark eyes as they rested upon her face and form.

"After that they were always together. In the mornings he was reading to her as she worked; on afternoons, rocking together in the little boat on the lake;

and then, in the purple twilight, singing dreamy German music, of which they were both passionately fond.

"I soon knew that James Alexander loved her. I read it in every glance, in every tone. But Eleanor? I was not sure. Watch her as narrowly as I would, I could not see that the rose in her cheek became a deeper pink when he approached, or that her eyes were raised more tenderly to him than to a dozen others who sought her smiles.

"There had been rumors of Eleanor's engagement and approaching marriage, which had drifted to me from her city home; but, when I saw her day by day allowing him to become more attached to her, — for she could not fail to perceive it all, — I rejected the rumor, and with it the impulse which had prompted me to repeat it to James, that he might, if not already too late, be upon his guard.

"At last the end came. I dozed one day on a sofa in an inner room, and watched with delicious delight my dream of fair woman that a dark-velvet lounging-chair brought out in clear relief. Eleanor sat there, with downcast eyes and clasped hands. Suddenly a step, hurried and joyous in its very lightness, sounded in the hall; the door opened and closed again, and Alexander stood before her with an open letter in his hand.

"'See,' he said, speaking rapidly, 'it has come at last, and I may speak. It is a call to one of the largest parishes in your own city, and I may say, what you must have known for weeks past, that I love you, Eleanor, deeply, devotedly; that I want you. My darling, tell me that you are not indifferent to me,—that you will be my wife.'

"It was too late for me to move; and something—perhaps it was a kind of dull despair—kept me motionless, with eyes riveted upon the group.

"'Speak to me, Eleanor,' he said, more eagerly, bending over her as he spoke.

"I saw her face flush, and an almost imperceptible shrinking from him, that made him quickly draw back.

"'Speak, Miss Orne,—Eleanor, I implore you.'

"'Oh, why have you said this to me?' she answered, faintly. 'I cannot hear you, Mr. Alexander. I am to be married next month.'

"I saw him reel for an instant as one would under a heavy blow, and heard a deep sigh—almost a groan—burst from him; then a silence so long and so profound that I could hear my heart beat. At last he spoke, in a voice husky and changed,—

"'Forgive me. I did not mean to offend; but God knows what a mercy it would have been if I could have known this before. I may touch your hand once,—may I not? And you will look up into my face? No, not that! Grant me this, at least then, before our long parting.' And he bent and kissed one of the sunny curls that streamed over the chair. Then I saw him raise one hand over her as in benediction, and, in another moment, he was gone. I looked at Eleanor. She had risen from her seat, and moved a step or two towards the door.

"'O James, James, I love you!' she said, piteously; and then I had just time to break her fall.

"An hour later, I met him on the door-step. 'I am glad to have seen you,' he said slowly, 'and to thank you for your kindness; for I am going away. You will be good to *her*, Anne, for my sake, — will you not?'

"He turned from me, and passed down the walk. I watched him until a sharp turn hid him from my sight. I never saw him afterwards alive.

"The next day it rained, and the next; and it was not until the third day that Eleanor and I took our usual walk. As we left the house, she suggested that we shape our way towards the lake. Agreeing, we walked on slowly, and I tried to make James Alexander the subject of our talk. At first she evaded me; and, when at last she found my persistence was not in any other way to be turned aside, said, —

"'It is an unpleasant subject to me, dear Anne. I fear I have much to blame myself for. *I* suffer enough; for, in rejecting his love, I shut my eyes on a life that would have been a continual delight, to open them on one from which my very soul shrinks abhorrently, and yet to which I am solemnly pledged.'

"'But it may not yet be too late,' I said, eagerly; for God knows I loved James Alexander with no selfish love.

"'Yes, it is too late,' she replied mournfully. 'I shall never allude to it again, Anne; but I tell you now, that

I do not and can never love Mr. Radnor; but there are family reasons that make the sacrifice of my hand a necessity. I never realized, until within the last few weeks, that it *was* such a sacrifice. I have been so happy, that I dared not break the spell by telling him the truth. And somehow the future seemed very far; and I did not dream that this summer would ever end.'

"Then there was silence between us for a space. At last she spoke again, —

"'I hope he will not suffer long. Tell him some time, Anne, what I have told you. He will not quite hate me, perhaps, then, if he knows that I was not drawing him on to gratify a foolish coquetry, but loved and suffered like himself.'

"I was about to reply, but she laid her hand on my mouth.

"'No,' she said. 'Let the subject go now forever. And no one will dream by-and-by how fair a love lies buried beneath my laces and jewels; or that, in the life of the noted man that he will one day surely become, is a romance that belongs to a dead past. It will all be the same a century hence. What does it matter after all?'

"But her words ended with a sigh that contrasted strangely with the forced lightness of her tone.

"Just then we came out of the grove, and could see far off the little waves of the lake dancing in the morning sunlight. I paused a moment to pick some late wild flowers, while Eleanor walked on quickly and disappeared among the alders that fringed the lake. I was following her slowly, when suddenly I heard one wild, thrilling cry, and then my name three times repeated. I flew almost down to the water, and there I saw Eleanor unconscious; and, close to the shore, among the lilies, — white and pure as their own petals, — a face upturned to the sky, swaying gently with the motion of the water. I need not tell you whose." Anne faltered.

"Do not go on," I said, with my own eyes and voice full of tears.

She raised her head quickly.

"I had schooled myself to it, dear, before I came, and I must finish. I am telling you of another's life, not mine.

"Then there was a brain fever for Eleanor, that no one believed she would ever rally from, in which she was either unconscious, or else singing snatches of German songs, with a pathos that was heart-rending.

"It was remarkable that neither to her mother nor to any one who watched over her did her words ever betray anything that could connect her illness with anything more than the bare horror of the discovery she made. She was married the next spring; and when I saw her, a month afterward, I should never, save for merest outline and coloring of beauty, have recognized her. Until last night, the past has never been alluded to by either of us. Then she confessed to me, that during the last ten years her life has been haunted by a perpetual remorse. The sun has set, dear, we will go home."

It was dusk when we crossed the pine grove, and the branches of the trees seemed, to my quickened imagination, to be singing a sad refrain to the story I had heard. We walked slowly, — Anne with head uplifted and a serene look upon her fair face that made me realize the refiner's work.

As we drew near the house there came forth a rolling symphony from the parlor organ, and then a voice that I had never heard before, in the *Agnus Dei* of the Twelfth Mass.

We paused, and Anne said quietly, — "She has never sung since he died until now."

We waited until the pure, pathetic tones had died away. Silence and the spirit of the hour was upon us. Overhead the large, calm stars hung low and bright. A gleam of light in Mrs. Radnor's rooms flashed for an instant, and disappeared; and a white figure came out upon the balcony of her apartment.

"Kyrie Eleison," said Anne, in a hushed voice. "Let us go in."

UNDER A CLOUD.

UNDER A CLOUD.

NE bitter cold day in January, four years ago, I had occasion to wait for a street-car in Chicago, on one of those aside lines where the cars pass but once in every ten or fifteen minutes. There was a German lager-bier saloon close by, and I entered it for shelter. As I stood by the stove, enjoying the grateful warmth, I observed near me a young man, in very seedy apparel, engaged in reading the *Staats-Zeitung*. Something in the air of the young man awakened my curiosity, and led me to address him. Although reading a German newspaper, he was not a German in appearance, and I put to him the question, "*Sind Sie Deutsch?*" by way of experiment.

"No, sir," he replied, "I am not German, but I speak and read the language."

I drew a chair near him, as he laid aside the newspaper, with the air of one willing to enter into conversation.

"Where did you pick up your German?" I asked.

"I picked it up," said the young man, with an air of

some pride in the statement, "where I picked up my Latin and Greek, — at college."

At this I ran my eye over him curiously. He had not the appearance of a scholar.

"You look surprised," said he. "Despite my present appearance, and the place you find me in, I am a graduate; but at present, I am under a cloud."

"So I should imagine."

I also imagined that the young man was probably shiftless, and no doubt addicted to liquor; but I did not say so. As if he read my thoughts, he spoke again:

"People are always ready to think ill of a seedy man, I suppose. Probably you think me a good-for-nothing, and would give me some valuable advice about hanging around beer-saloons; but the fact is, I am an employé of this establishment."

He spoke with a bitter irony, that ill-concealed a sort of shame in the confession.

"May I ask in what capacity?" said I.

"You may, sir; and I may answer or not, I suppose. I think I will decline to answer. As I said, I am under a cloud. I am not proud of my employment, but I do what I do because I can't do better, and idleness is synonymous with hunger and cold for me and mine."

"You are married, then?"

"Yes, sir," — with sudden reserve.

"Don't be offended at my inquisitiveness," said I. "I spoke to you first out of mere curiosity, it is true; but I speak now out of interest in you. If I could help you, I would. There is my card."

He took it with a respectful inclination of the head.

"I've heard of you," said he, as he glanced at the name. "I can't give you my card, sir, because I don't own such a thing." He smiled. "My name is Brock St. John."

"I hear the car coming," said I. "I'll see you again, Mr. St. John. I don't set up for a philanthropist; but I like to do a good turn when I can. Good-morning."

And I went my own way.

Henry Kingsley, — or rather a character of his creation, — in one of his novels, remarks that he suspects there is some of the poetical faculty about him, because he is accustomed to walk out of nights when anything goes wrong.

This is also my case.

To "fetch a walk" about the streets, late in the evening, has long been a favorite antidote for trouble with me. When the night is stormy, the value of this remedy for fretting cares is tenfold increased. There is an exhilarating sense of power in overcoming the opposing forces of the elements, and breasting along at a brisk pace against a furious storm of sleet or rain. As Leigh Hunt said, you have a feeling of respect for your legs under such circumstances; you admire their toughness as they propel you along in the teeth of the storm. As your blood begins to warm up, and to whirl through your veins with an exhilaration beside which that of wine is tame and effeminate, the "blues" that have been gibing you vanish like magic. Always, after such a bout, I return home and "sleep like a top," no matter what discomforts or sorrows have been running their sleep-dispelling race through my head before starting out.

On the night of the day that I met St. John I started out about eleven o'clock for such a walk. The winds were holding high carnival that night, and a fierce storm of mingled hail and rain swept through the almost deserted streets. I forged along (as the sailors say), with my head down, block after block, fighting the forces of nature, with the same pleasure that Victor Hugo's hero felt, no doubt, in like effort. True, my fight was to his as a cock-fight is to an encounter of lions; but the limit of power is the limit of delight in overcoming in any case. The boy who declaims "the Roman Soldier" at school to the rapture of his gaping audience is as happy in his achievement as the tragedian who thrills a theatreful. Gilliatt conquered storms, and so did I; he was on the high seas, and I was in the streets of Chicago.

Sounds of music and dancing fell on my ear. They came from the beer-saloon of the morning. Curiosity impelled me to enter.

The air was reeking with tobacco-smoke and the fumes of lager-bier. The seats about the half-dozen tables were crowded with Teutonic guzzlers; and, at the lower part of the room there was a cleared space where a half-dozen couples were whirling in a waltz with that thorough abandon which characterizes your

German in his national dance. On a slightly raised platform against the wall was a band composed of a violin, a clarionet, and a trombone.

The violinist was my acquaintance of the morning.

He caught sight of me as I elbowed my way toward the dancing-floor, and blushed violently. Then an expression of angry pride settled on his countenance, and he continued his playing with stolid indifference to my gaze.

When the dance was over (and St. John kept up the music till the surprised Teutons who played the wind-instruments were sheer worn-out with their prolonged exertions), I went up to the young man, and shook hands with him.

"At work, eh?" I remarked, with a miserable effort to seem cheerful and easy.

"Yes, sir. You have found me out. You know now how I keep the wolf from my door."

"Yes, Mr. St. John; and I do not forget that it *is* to keep the wolf from your door. Still, I hope you are thoroughly misplaced here, — I *hope* you are!"

He grasped my hand with a quick, strong pressure.

"I must prove to you that I am, that's all," said he; "come to — to where I live, to-morrow, and let me tell you the whole story."

He took my pencil and wrote the address in my note-book.

"To-morrow afternoon," said I, "I will call."

The next day I found my way to the wretched tenement house in North Clark street, where St. John lived, and climbed three pair of stairs to the door of his room. I rapped, and the young man opened the door.

I have seen a good deal of poverty in my day, and I was prepared to find it here, as I did. But I was not prepared for the sight of such a beautiful young face as that which met my gaze here, and to the possessor of which St. John introduced me as his wife. She seemed like some little girl that was lost. The unmistakable air of the true lady showed itself in every detail of her dress and manner,—in the small, white collar at the neck of the calico dress, in the smooth-banded hair that matched the brown eyes, in the quiet demeanor that told of natural and unconscious self-respect. It showed itself, too, in the perfect neatness of the room, in which there was a cheerful, home-like air, despite the poor and barren nature of its furnishings. The room was kitchen and bedroom, dining-room and sitting-room, in one; but the bed was smooth and clean, and the little cooking-stove was without spot.

Mrs. St. John was engaged in the unpoetic occupation of mending her husband's only coat. He was in his shirt-sleeves.

"Aggie expected to get the coat done before our guest came," said St. John, with a smile. "If you are at all particular, I'll put it on with the needle sticking in it, and she can finish it after you are gone. But I am accustomed to sitting in my shirt-sleeves."

"So am I," was my reply; and, accordingly, I pulled off my own coat, and sat in my shirt-sleeves, too. In the act, my cigar-case fell out of my pocket.

"Light a cigar, sir, if you like," said St. John, with a brisk assumption of the airs of a genial host; "my wife don't allow me to smoke, but my guests always do. She is fond of cigars, is Aggie."

The little wife looked up with a demure and childlike air.

"He never offers to smoke, sir," said she, "because"—

"Because I can't afford it," put in St. John. "I was a great smoker in college; but those were my wild days. Thank you."

The last remark was in acknowledgment of an offered cigar. We were soon puffing great cloud-wreaths toward the ceiling, and an air of restraint that had rested on us at first, despite our efforts to avoid it, was speedily vanished. Cigars are social.

"And now, sir," said St. John, "you shall hear the story I promised you. I hope it wont bore you."

"If it does I'll cry out," said I.

The little wife laughed quietly.

"I graduated; I married; I came to Chicago," began St. John, sententiously.

"*Veni, vidi, vici,*" said I.

"Quite the contrary; I *was* conquered. I had that idea which young men from the east, just out of college, are apt to have, that in this great western city there was a comparative lack of intellectual culture, and that a man of my education must speedily and easily get into a position of prominence, where my talents would earn me a fine living. But I very soon found where my mistake lay. I had not been bred to work,—real, practical, marketable work,—either mental or physical. The professions were open to me, as to any other beginner,—nothing more. I could not step out of college into a lucrative practice at the bar; but I could enter a law-office, and study. So of the other professions. If I had any one idea more prominent than another, it was that I could secure an editorial situation at once on one of the newspapers here. I was surprised to find that there was absolutely no demand for such services as I had to offer.

"'Do you know anything about the newspaper business?' was the first question put to me, by the first publisher to whom I made application.

"That was the very last question that I had expected to have asked of me. Of course I imagined myself competent, or I should not have applied for editorial employment; but I knew the publisher meant, Had I had actual experience on the press? I felt so sure of myself that I was tempted to answer him 'Yes,' but the fact is I was never brought up with such a reverence for the truth, as to always keep at a respectful distance from it; so I told him I had not, but I could quickly learn.

"'We are in no need of students,' said he; 'and, even if we took you to teach you, your pay would not settle your washing-bill.'

"One editor was good enough to let me try my hand at writing a political article. I sat down in his sanctum and went to work. At the end of two hours I handed him what I had written, quite confident that I had settled the question of utility. It was an essay that would have brought me honor at college. He read it and smiled.

"'I don't want to hurt your feelings at all," said he, 'but you have been two hours about a piece of work that a ready writer would knock off in half an hour, and now it is done it is good for nothing. You make the mistake so many have made before you, that an editor does not need to be bred to his business. *My* alma mater was a printing-office,' said he, proudly, 'and I crept up the ladder round by round. When I commenced editorial labor, I dropped type-setting, at which I earned two dollars a day, to handle the reporter's pencil at seven dollars a week. If you think you could do anything as a reporter, I'll show you our Mr. Pyke, the local editor.'

"Mr. Pyke was a rough one.

"'Posted around town,' said he.

"I told him I was a new-comer.

"'Know short-hand?'

"'No, sir.'

"'What line are you strongest in?'

"What line?' said I, not exactly understanding.

"'Yes, what line? Speeches, fancy-work, police, sensations, picking up items around town — or what?'

"'I really don't know,' said I; 'I've never had any experience, practically, in the newspaper business.'

"At this Mr. Pyke turned round on me with a queer look in his face.

"'Oh, that's it,' said he; 'you want to work at a trade you haven't served an apprenticeship to. There! it's the old story. If you'll go up in the composing-room, they'll give you a stick and put you to setting type, I reckon. You better try it. Go and ask for our foreman, Mr. Buckingham, and tell him I sent you,—will you? Why, you couldn't tell where the *e* box is!'

"The man's manner was not so rude as his language, sir. He seemed perfectly good-natured, and was scribling away with a lead-pencil all the while he was talking, much as if he were a writing-machine."

"Doubtless he is, to a great degree," said I; "that is just where the apprenticeship does its work. I know Pyke, and I've seen him write a column of city matter, carrying on conversations with half-a-dozen different people who dropped in during the time, without interrupting him at all. But I don't mean to interrupt *you;* go on, please."

"Well, sir," St. John continued, "before I had thoroughly learned the lesson that I finally learned so well, I was almost literally penniless. Such had been my high confidence in the easy and prosperous path before me in Chicago, that when I came here I took board at a first-class hotel, with my wife. I had very little money, and one day I waked up to the consciousness that I had less than five dollars remaining of that little, and still no work. Two hideous gulfs yawned before me,—starvation and debt. My horror of the one is scarcely greater than my horror of the other. Debt converted my father from a well-to-do man into a bankrupt, and my mother, who owns the little that is left of our old homestead in Massachusetts, was and is in no condition to help me. I would beg in the streets, sir, before I would look to my poor mother for help, after the long years of self-denial she practised to get me through college. My wife is an orphan. You may judge the color my future was taking on. I left the Tremont House, and, falling at once from the highest to the lowest style of living in apartments, came *here*. I had no confidence left, now, in that future which had before seemed, so foolish and inexperienced was I, a broad and flowery path for talent and education to tread. I never intend to whine over anything in this world if I can help it, but I can assure you this was a pretty dark old world to Brock St. John about that time. The prospect of earning a dollar a day would have cheered me wonderfully. I cared more on account of Aggie than myself, of course. A man can bear ups and downs, kicks, cold shoulders, and an empty stomach, if he is alone; but the thought that I have dragged *her* down to this is almost unbearable at times."

"You have *not* dragged me, Brock," spoke up the little wife; "I came of my own accord!"

"That you did, Aggie," said the husband, his eyes moistening; "I am slandering you. But to go on: The day after we moved in here, and set up house-keeping in careful preparation for the cold winter coming (I had to pawn clothing to get these poor goods," he added, looking about the room with a smile), "the German musician, who lives next door, came in to ask us if his practising on a trombone annoyed us. We were so hungry for a friendly face just then, that we would have let the good-natured German blow his trombone through our transom-window after that exhibition of fellow-feeling. That afternoon, I dropped in to see him, in continuance of the acquaintance. There was a violin hanging on the wall, and I took it down and played a tune on it.

That was my introduction to my first situation in Chicago. Stumm got me my place at the beer-saloon; and so, through the knowledge of an art which has always been to me nothing more than an amusement, I get enough to live, in this time when all the hard-earned culture, which cost me so much labor, fails me utterly. I am thankful for this, heartily thankful; but I don't need to tell you sir, how it galls me to do this work, — to sit three or four hours of every evening in a dense and vulgar atmosphere, fiddling for my daily bread. No wonder I am seedy; no wonder I get to look like a loafer, listless, without pride, spite of Aggie's wifely care. If I knew an honest trade, I should be a happy man. I would gladly barter my knowledge of Latin, Greek, and German for the knowledge of type-setting."

"So that you could prove to Pyke that you know the *e* box from the *x* box?" queried I.

He laughed.

"But you talk the words of bitterness when you talk in that way, St. John. You can barter your knowledge of German for *cash*, and keep it too. Have you ever sought for pupils!"

"Only a little. I have no acquaintances, you know. My only way to get pupils was to advertise, of course. I tried it three days, and got not a solitary reply. There are scores of teachers advertising. It seemed useless for me to waste money in that way."

"Well," said I, "I think I can set you in a way of getting up a class. My own German is very rusty, and I will be pupil number one. Then I know of two or three friends who want to study the language. I think we can get you up a class among us."

He made me no protestation of gratitude, — such protestations are usually humbug, — but I saw his gladness in his face.

The little wife sat squeezing her fingers for joy.

Before a month had passed, St. John had a large class in German, and bade adieu to fiddling. He proved an excellent teacher. Long before I left Chicago to resume my residence in this city, he had got nicely out from under his cloud, and was living in a snug house in the West Division.

There was a little baby playing on the floor at his house last summer when I called to see him, on my way to Lake Superior. That baby bears my name, I am proud to say.

COMING FROM THE FRONT.

Coming from the Front.

"Head-Quarters, Dep't and Army of the Tennessee.
" *East Point, Georgia, September* 22, 1864.
"SPECIAL ORDERS.
"No. 214.

[EXTRACT.]

. . . .

"XI. Having tendered his resignation, the following-named officer is honorably discharged from the military service of the United States, with condition that he shall receive no final payments until he satisfies the Pay Department that he is not indebted to the Government.

"1st Lieut. —— ——, Ills. Vol. Inf'try.

"By order of Maj. Gen'l O. O. Howard.

"(Signed) W. T. Clark, *Ass't Adj't Gen'l.*"

THINK of that! After forty-one months of hard-tack and hard marching, interspersed with enough fighting to satisfy the stomach of an ordinary man; after so long an experience of the beautiful uncertainty of army life; after polluting, with the invading heel of my brogan, the sacred soil of several of our erring sister States; after passing many breezy and rainy nights under the dubious shelter of shelter-tents; after sitting through long and weary days in the furnace-heat of narrow and dirty trenches; — after all this, I am at last permitted to bid farewell to "the front," to go home and doff the honorable blue for the more sober garb of the "cit," and drop into my wonted insignificance. That little "extract" has a sweeter perfume for me than any triple extract for the handkerchief ever elaborated by the renowned M. Lubin. It is fragrant with thoughts of home and loved ones far away in the Northland, of starry nights and starry eyes, of fluttering fans and floating drapery, of morning naps unbroken by the strident *ra-tata-ta-ta* of the bugle. I grow quite sentimental over it, notwithstanding the unpleasant condition with which it is qualified, and which involves such a fearful amount of writing and figuring on mysterious close-ruled blanks, and so much affidavit-making and other swearing, — especially at the blundering clerks in the departments at Washington.

But this troubles me little now. Time enough to attend to it after I get home. That is all I can think of, — *home*, and how to get there.

How I should get there, and whether or not I ever would get there, were questions not easily solved. It is the purpose of this sketch to show some of the beauties of travelling on railroads that are under military control, and especially to set forth the writer's experience in going from Atlanta to Nashville.

It was a terribly hot morning when I reached the depot at Atlanta, amid a cloud of dust and a maze of wagons and mules and commissary stores and frantic teamsters. I threw my valise into the nearest car and hastened to the Provost Marshal's office for my pass. There was an anxious crowd already in waiting: resigned officers and officers on leave; jolly, ragged privates on furlough, eager to see their wives and babies; sutlers and "sheap-cloding" men; flaring demireps, seeking new fields; mouldy citizens in clothes of antique cut, fawning abjectly and addressing every clerk and orderly as "kernel;" dejected darkies, shoved aside by everybody, with no "civil rights bill" to help them. While I was waiting for my turn, the train kept me constantly worried by pulling up and backing down and threatening to leave. At last I found an opportunity to exhibit my "Extract," and, after reading it as slowly and carefully as if it had been a dispatch in cipher, the Provost Marshal very deliberately wrote a pass, read it over two or three times, and then, looking at every one in the room but me, asked "Who's this for?" as if I had not been standing at his elbow with my hand held out for half an hour.

I left the official premises in a highly exasperated state of mind. In the mean time the train had been plunging backward and forward in a wild and aimless way, and I was unable to find the car my valise was in. After much wear and tear of muscle and temper and trousers, in climbing over boxes and bales of hay, I discovered it, and found that it had been taken possession of by a crowd of roystering blades on furlough, whose canteens were full and fragrant, and in whose talk and manner appeared the signs of a boisterous night ahead, with the possibility of a fight or two by way of special diversion. As I was no longer in "the military service of the United States," I was, of course, a peaceable citizen, so I took my quarters in a more peaceful car. It was a cattle-car and not remarkably clean; but the company was good, and through the lattice-work around the upper part of the car one could get a view of the surrounding country; though looking through it gave one a sensation very much like being in a guard-house.

"Will we never get off?" was the question asked dozens of times, — asked of nobody in particular, and answered by a chorus of incoherent growls from everybody in general, while some humorous young man suggested that if any one wanted to get off, he'd better do it before the train started.

"Now we're off!"

"No we're not," said the humorous young man, "but it's more'n likely we will be before we get to Chattanooga."

This was not particularly encouraging to timid travellers, in a country abounding in guerrilleroes, and where accident insurance companies were unknown.

Between Atlanta and Marietta we passed line after line of defensive works, protected by *abattis* and *chevaux-de-frise*, — feed-racks, I heard a bronzed veteran of rural antecedents call them, — built by the rebels at night, only to be abandoned on the next night to the great

Flanker. While they wrought line upon line, Sherman and his boys in blue gave them precept upon precept, here a little and there a great deal. All this rugged country is historic ground. The tall, tufted pine-trees stand as monuments of the unrecorded dead, and every knoll and tangled ravine bears witness to a bravery and heroic endurance that has never been surpassed.

Leaving Marietta, — deserted by its inhabitants and turned into an immense hospital, — we approached Kenesaw, so lately crowned with cannon and alive with gray coats, now basking in the afternoon sunlight, as quiet and harmless as a good-natured giant taking his after-dinner nap. We approached it from the inside, to gain which side the compact columns of Logan and Stanley and Davis hurled themselves against its rugged front so fearlessly, but, alas, so fruitlessly, on that terrible 27th of June.

Farther on we came to Alatoona Pass, taken at first without a struggle, but afterward baptized in blood and made glorious by a successful defence against immense odds.

It was sunset when we reached Kingston, — a straggling row of dilapidated shanties. As the train was to stop some time, I started out in search of supper. There was no hotel, so I had to depend upon sutlers, or peripatetic venders of pies. I entered one sutler's store, and found a few fly-specked red handkerchiefs and some suspenders. Another contained nothing but combs and shoe-blacking. Turning away mournfully, I espied an aged colored man limping up the street with a basket on his arm. I rushed madly at him, and, finding that he had apple-pies, was soon the happy possessor of a brace of them. I congratulated myself and gratefully sat down upon a stone to eat, and — well, *such pies!* It was utterly impossible to tell what the crust was made of. In taste and toughness it resembled a dirty piece of towel. The interior — "the bowels of the thing," as some one inelegantly called it, — consisted of a few slices of uncooked immature apple and a great many flies cooked whole. The cooks were altogether too liberal with their flies. I am not particularly well versed in the culinary art myself, but I venture boldly to say that the flies that were in those two pies would have sufficed, if judiciously distributed, to season two dozen pies with the same proportion of apple in them.

And of such was my supper at Kingston. The whistle sounded, and we got aboard and were off for Chattanooga.* Night fell peacefully upon Kingston and its dirty peddlers of unwholesome pies, as a curve in the road hid it and them from our reproachful gaze.

As the darkness increased, and we went dashing at break-neck speed over a road that had had little or no care bestowed upon it since the opening of the campaign, I thought of the humorous young man's remark, and of how unpleasant and inconvenient it would be to have this long train thrown off and its contents, as Meister Karl hath it, "pepperboxically distributed" in the adjacent ditch.

And then to have one of Wheeler's men take advantage of a fellow, as he lay there with a broken leg, and rob him of the few dollars he had borrowed to go home on! Well, we had been taking our chances for the last three years, and it was no new thing to take them now. With this comforting reflection, I sat down on my valise, and, wrapped in my great-coat, awaited the coming of "the balmy." It was rather unsatisfactory waiting. Something in my head kept going rattlety-bang, jerkety-jerk, bumpety-bump, in unison with the noise of the cars; and when I did get into a doze, I was harassed by the dim shadow of a fear that we were about to leave the track and go end-over-end down an embankment. At last weariness overcame me, and I slept soundly, half-lying on the dirty floor, half-leaning on my valise, coiled up in one of those attitudes in which only an old campaigner can sleep at all. I woke amid an unearthly whizzing of steam, to find the train standing still, and myself mysteriously entangled with various arms and legs that didn't belong to me. I extricated myself and looked out. Through the thick darkness of the early morning there glared upon me the light of what seemed to be innumerable fierce, unwinking eyes. I began to think that I had taken the wrong train and brought up in the lower regions; but a little reflection and rubbing of the eyes disclosed to me that we had reached Chattanooga in safety, and that those fierce eyes were the head-lights of the locomotives that had arrived during the night, and were now blowing off their superfluous steam in that wild, unearthly manner. As soon as it was daylight I inquired about trains going North, and learned that there was no telling when a train would go, as Forrest was said to be in the neighborhood of the road. So there was nothing to do but to go to the Crutchfield House and wait. Alas for the man whose purse is slim, under any circumstances! Alas and alas for him if he was obliged to wait in Chattanooga at Crutchfield prices! It was a dollar that he had to pay for each scanty meal, a dollar for the use of a densely populated bed, and a dollar must be deposited with the clerk to secure the return of the little towel he wiped his face on. Besides the pecuniary depletion that he suffered, he was bored to death with weary waiting, with nothing to do and nowhere to go. Chattanooga was far from being a cheerful place, especially in the rainy season, when nothing was visible out of doors except the lonesome sentinels pacing their beats in dripping ponchos, and with guns tucked under their arms, and here and there a team of steaming mules, struggling to draw a creaking, lumbering wagon through the detestable clay.

For amusement, there was a billiard-room, where one had to wait eight hours for a chance to play. If he failed to see any fun in this, he could step into another room, and squander his currency for, and bemuddle his brains with, a sloppy sort of beverage that the gentlemanly proprietor would assure him was good, new beer. I would rather take his word than his beer. At night, if his tastes ran that way, for a small outlay one could witness what was called a dramatic exhibition, but which was really more anatomical than dramatic.

In this enlivening village, an ever-increasing crowd of us was compelled to wait for five long days. Resigned officers were far from being resigned, and officers on leave were vexed and impatient because it was impossible to leave.

At length the joyful news spread that a train would leave for Nashville at two o'clock in the afternoon. I rushed to the depot, and was just fairly aboard a car, when some one, more forcibly than politely, told me to "git out o' that car." As he spoke as a man who had authority, and knew it, I got out, and learned that I was on the wrong train, and in a fair way to have been carried to Knoxville. I forgave the man his abruptness of speech, and went in search of the right train. Catching a glimpse of Capt. S., whom I knew to be going North, in one of the cars, I got in without farther question; and soon a fearful jerk, that piled us like deadwood in one end of the car, started us towards Nashville. Rattling along at the usual reckless rate, we found ourselves, soon after dark, at Stevenson, Alabama. Here we were to stay all night; for the managers of affairs still had the fear of Forrest before their eyes, and dared not run trains at night. It was raining, and the darkness of Erebus covered the face of the earth. Notwithstanding this, Capt. S. and myself plunged out into the night, determined to get something to eat, or perish in the attempt. After wandering blindly for a while,—

tumbling into ditches, and falling over boxes and barrels, that turned up where they were least expected,—we finally brought up among the ropes of the tent of a sutler. We entered, and found the proprietor dozing over a dime novel. We were sorry to disturb him in his literary pursuits; but we were hungry, and had to be fed. We eagerly demanded various articles of food, which he sleepily informed us he hadn't got. Questioning him closely as to the edible part of his stock in trade, we learned that it consisted of some Boston crackers and a little cheese. We filled our haversacks with these, regardless of expense. Having bought so generously, the proprietor became generous in turn, and, bringing forth a square black bottle, proffered it to us with the remark: "You'll find that a leetle the best gin this side o' Louisville. Take hold!" The captain took hold; but the silent, though expressive comment, that was written on his countenance when he let go, induced me to decline with thanks. A decent regard for the man's feelings prevented any audible expression; but, as soon as we were out of the tent, the captain solemnly assured me that he was poisoned, and that he would utter his last words when he got comfortably fixed in the car. Getting back to the car was almost as perilous an undertaking as finding the sutler's store; but, fortunately, we were guided by the voice of Capt. W. crying, in heart-rending tones, "Lost child! lost child!" Capt. S. interrupted one of his most pathetic cries by striking him in the pit of the stomach with a loaded haversack, and demanding to be helped aboard. Once more snugly ensconced in our car, we proceeded to sup right royally on our crackers and cheese. S. forgot all about his last words until some time near the middle of the night, when he woke me to say that he had concluded to postpone them till he got home, where he could have them published in the county paper. Barring this interruption, I slept soundly all night, having more room than on the trip from Atlanta, and not having the thunder of a running train sounding in my ears.

At breakfast-time we drew out the fragmentary remainder of our last night's repast, and were about to take our morning meal, when we discovered that both crackers and cheese had a singularly animated appearance. Symptoms of internal commotion manifested themselves in all of us except S., who thought that, as the gin had not killed him, he was proof against anything. His stoic composure acted soothingly upon the rest of us, and we concluded that it was too late to feel bad, and consoled each other by repeating the little rhyme, —

"What can't be cured
Must be endured."

By eight o'clock the fog lifted, and we started on our journey northward. Wild and contradictory stories were afloat in regard to the whereabouts and doings of the terrible, ubiquitous Forrest. Revolvers were brought out and capped and primed afresh, and watches and rings were hidden in what were deemed inaccessible parts of the clothing. There was considerable anxiety in regard to the bridges over Elk and Duck rivers, and when we had passed them both safely, the train quickened its speed, every one breathed more freely, and the belligerent men put away their fire-arms.

We hastened on without accident and with decreasing fear, though the *débris* of broken and burned cars that lined the roadside, suggesting some unpleasant reflections, and at the close of the day entered the picket lines at Nashville, and were safe.

Then came a foot-race, from the depot to the hotel, for a prize that nobody won, for all the hotels in the city were already full from cellar to garret. Capt. S. and I sat down upon the cold, hard curb-stone and mingled our weary groans, while W., more plucky and better acquainted with the city, went in search of a boarding-house. Having returned, with the cheering intelligence that he had found beds and supper, we followed him gladly, and, after eating a supper, the quantity of which I would not like to confess, retired to our rooms, and were soon — to use the captain's elegant language — "wrapped in that dreamless, refreshing slumber that only descends upon the pillow of the innocent and beautiful."

A NIGHT IN THE SEWERS.

A NIGHT IN THE SEWERS.

PERHAPS some of my fair readers will consider me a disagreeable person for telling them something I know about kid gloves. Perhaps they will not believe me when I tell them that in Paris and elsewhere there exists — or did exist not very long ago — an extensive trade in the skins of common rats, and that these skins, when dressed and dyed, are converted into those delicate coverings for the hands, commonly called "kid" gloves, and supposed to be manufactured from the hides of immature goats.

I was acquainted with a dog-dealer in Paris, a Dane, whose name was Beck. To him I went one day, bent upon obtaining a terrier dog of good intellect and agreeable manners, who should be a companion to me in my "lodgings for single gentlemen," and whose gambols might serve to amuse me in my lighter hours, when, after work, I would make little pedestrian excursions in the neighborhood, for the sake of exercise and air. Beck's kennel was comprised in a small yard, at the back of a rickety house; and, when I entered it, persuasion was hardly needed to induce me to stand as near the centre of the enclosure as possible, in order to keep at chain's length from what the French call *boule dogues*, several of which ill-looking canines formed a portion of Beck's stock in trade.

"Here," said Mr. Beck, in reply to a question of mine and in pretty good English, "here in this box I have a small dog of a kind quite fashionable now. They call him a Skye terrier, and I have given him the name of 'Dane,' because he comes from far north, like myself, and has long yellow hair."

With these words, Mr. Beck laid hold of a chain, and drawing it sharply, jerked out from among some straw a creature made up, apparently, of tow and wire, with a pair of eyes like black beads glittering through the shocks of hair that fell over its head. The animal seemed cowed, and I did not think much of him at first sight.

"He has had bad usage," said Mr. Beck; "first time I saw him was yesterday, when he burst in at my back-door, with a horse-shoe fastened to his tail. There, you see I have nailed the shoe over the door of his box. He will be a lucky bargain for whoever buys him, you may depend upon that."

"Good upon rats?" asked I.

"Know nothing about him," replied Mr. Beck, honestly; "never saw him before yesterday. They all take the water kindly though, these Skyes do, and if you want to try him at rats, I can put you in the way of it."

Somehow I took to the ragged little beast, and so I paid Mr. Beck sixty francs for him, and ten more for the little wooden kennel with the horseshoe nailed upon it. I have a great regard for horseshoes as insurers of luck; because once, when I had picked up one on the road, and carried it home in my pocket, I found a letter on my table, informing me that I had come in for a small legacy, through the death of an aged kinswoman whom I had never seen.

What with good treatment and diet, the frequent bath and the free use of the comb, it was not many days before master Dane became a very presentable dog, and had quite recovered his pluck and spirits. He bullied, and banished forever to the house-top, a large tortoise-shell cat, that had hitherto commanded the garrison, and I thought, one day, that I should like to try him at rats. So out I sallied with him in search of Mr. Beck, who had promised to put me in the way of getting some sport of the kind.

That versatile gentleman was not in his kennel when I called, but his wife told me that I would find him in the "skinnery" attached to the establishment; and, asking me to follow her, she ushered me into a long, low apartment, lighted with a row of circular windows. The odor of the place was very pungent and disagreeable. There were several wooden tanks ranged along one wall of the room, and, on lines stretched along by the windows, a number of small skins were hung to dry. Mr. Beck, assisted by a couple of tan-colored boys, was busily engaged in stirring the contents of the tanks. A dead rat on the floor immediately engaged the attention of Dane, who seized it in his teeth, shook it savagely for a moment, and then pitched it away from him, apparently in disgust at finding it already dead.

"What do you make of the rat-skins?" inquired I, after I had looked on for a while.

"Money," rejoined Mr. Beck, curtly; "but the man I dress them for makes them into gloves, — ladies' gloves, of the primest quality."

"Ladies have rats about them in more ways than one, then," said I. "Where do you get the raw material?"

"The rat-hunters supply me. Their hunting-grounds lie all under the streets of Paris. Would you like to have a day in the sewers with your terrier? Simonet will be here in a few minutes, and you can go the rounds with him if you will."

Just what I wanted, and so I sat upon a bench and waited, and presently a man came in. He was a low-sized, squat fellow of about forty, with heavy, round shoulders, and bowed legs; and his head and face were almost entirely covered with a thatch of tangled red hair, out from which there peered a couple of greenish eyes of very sinister expression. He had a leathern sack slung over his shoulder, and carried in his hand a long wand of birch, brushy, with the twigs left upon it at one end.

"On the rounds, eh, Simonet?" said Mr. Beck, addressing this agreeable-looking gentleman; "well, here's a monsieur who would like to go with you. He wants to try his terrier at the rats. You can make your own bargain with him."

Then looking at me, he continued, —

"Better leave your coat with my old woman, who'll give you a clean *blouse* instead."

Madame took my coat, and gave me a strong *blouse* and a somewhat greasy cap; and in this guise I went forth with Simonet, who immediately plunged into the thick of the city slums. After having gone some distance, we entered a dismal and dirty office, in which a man, turning over some piles of documents, after a few whispered words with my guide, handed him a bunch of heavy keys, and we again went out into the streets. Entering a paved court-yard, a declivity led us down to a sort of tunnel, the entrance to which was barred by a heavy, grated door, which Simonet opened with one of the keys, locking it again as soon as we had got in.

"We are in one of the main sewers now, monsieur," said he, in a squeaky, rat-like voice; "you must be careful to keep close by me, and not stray away into any of the branches."

It was pitch dark, as I looked before me into the tunnel, — dark, and awful, and silent, but for the gliding, oozing sound of slowly-flowing water. Simonet produced a lantern, which he lit, and I could see by the dim light thrown from it that we were in a vast stone passage, through the centre of which there ran a dark, deep stream. Between the wall and the stream on either side there was a broad pathway, or ledge, and along this the rat-hunter motioned me to follow him. Soon we reached a turn in the tunnel, and here Simonet, after searching about upon the wall for a moment, found a rusty nail in it, upon which he hung his lantern. Then producing a couple of torches from his sack, he lighted them, and handed one to me.

"There is a birch wattle hid away somewhere here," said he, — "ah, yes! — here it is, take it monsieur, and use it just as you shall see me do when we get among the rats. Keep close to me, else you may get lost in the drains."

Dane grew very excited, now, and ran ahead of us a good way, and presently we heard a great rushing and squeaking, and the suppressed snarling of the little dog as he worried the rats. Then we saw many rats running hither and thither, some of them so scared by the light of the torches, as they came near us, that they leaped into the water, while others ran up the wall, from which we quickly knocked them with our wattles. Simonet did not put them into his bag, but left them where they fell, saying that his custom was to pick them up on his way back.

The dog behaved wonderfully well, fighting and shaking the rats that fell in his way with great fierceness and pluck. At last, when we had killed about a hundred of them, we thought it time to rest. Simonet produced a short, black pipe, and, as I was filling mine, he cast a wistful look at my tobacco-pouch, thinking, probably, that the article contained in it must be of a quality superior to that of the cheap stuff smoked by him ; so I poured half the contents of it into his hand, and he filled his pipe from it, with a grin of satisfaction on his ugly face.

"It will soon be time for us to turn back," said he, after a while; "the best place for rats is a little way further on, and it will be too late to try it if we don't go forward now."

On we went, slashing right and left at the rats, most of which, I noticed, were of a very black color here, as if belonging to a peculiar colony that existed in this part of the tunnel. As we rounded a corner, however, a very large white rat ran past us, and disappeared down a cross-gallery that led away to the left. Wishing to secure this animal as a trophy, I hallooed the terrier upon its tracks, and was about following the chase, when Simonet laid his hand upon my arm, and whispered, in a tone of entreaty,—

"Don't risk your life, monsieur ! He who follows the white rat of the sewer is likely never to find his way back alive. There's a blight about the creature, and old stories are afloat of how it has led rat-hunters away into dangerous parts of the sewers, like a jack-o'-lantern, and then set upon them with a number of its kind, and picked their bones clean ! "

Breaking away from the fellow, with a jerk that knocked the pipe out of his hand, and sent it spinning into the black water below, I ran down the by-sewer after the terrier, whose whimper, as though he were yet in full chase, I could hear at a good distance ahead of me. When I came up with him, which I did only after having taken several turns, he seemed at fault, head up and tail down, and gazing, with a very puzzled expression up at the vaulted roof. There was no white rat to be seen, nor could I detect any aperture in the walls, into which the creature could have made its escape. Then a sort of superstitious fear fell upon me, as I thought of Simonet's warning, and, with a word of encouragement to the dog, I hastened to retrace my steps, shouting loudly every now and then, so as to let the rat-hunter know of my whereabouts. But no responsive halloo came to my call. Not a sound was to be heard but the hollow beat of my footsteps on the damp, mouldy path, and the squeaking, here and there, of the rats, as we disturbed them from their feast on some garbage fished up by them from the slimy bed of the drain. Excited at the position in which I found myself, I now began to make reckless *détours* hither and thither, until, thoroughly exhausted by my exertions, I leaned my back against the wall, and tried to remember such marks as might have been observed by me in the tunnel since I had parted from Simonet. The only marks of the wayside that I could recall, however, were the dead rats left by us upon the ledge as we passed, and of these I had seen none while I was trying to retrace my steps. Arguing from this, and from the fact that Simonet did not respond to my shouts, which I continued to utter at intervals, I began to feel an extremely unpleasant nervous shiver creeping over me, suggestive of all the horrors about which I had ever read or dreamed. The little dog lay cowering at my feet, as if he, too, were somewhat dejected at the prospect of being eaten alive by avenging rats; and, to crown the situation, just as I had nerved myself for another effort to recover the lost clue, my torch went out with a malignant flicker, and I found myself in black darkness!

Sinking down at the foot of the wall, I now gave myself up for lost. Even had the torch not been quite burnt out, I had no means of relighting it, having used my last match when we stopped to smoke, just before I broke away from my guide. I think I must have become somewhat delirious now; for I have a faint recollection of wild songs chanted, and of yells that made the vaulted roof ring again. Then a heavy sleep must have fallen upon me, which probably lasted for several hours; and then I awoke to a dim consciousness of horror, as I began to realize the terrible situation into which I had brought myself by my reckless folly. My dog was still nestling close to me; and it may have been to his presence, perhaps, that I owed the fact of my not having been mangled by rats during my sleep. Rising with difficulty to my feet, for I was stiff from lying so long upon the damp, cold ground, I once more tried to shout; but my voice was utterly gone, from my previous exertion of it, and I could not raise it above a whisper. Then, in sheer desperation, I dragged myself along the wall, feeling the way with my hands, and had not gone many paces when I felt an angle in the masonry, on rounding which a ray of hope dawned upon me, as I discerned a faint light, far, far away, at the end of what seemed to be all but an endless shaft of darkness. The prospect of escape infused new vigor into my weary limbs, and I kept steering onward for the light, which grew larger and larger as I approached it. At last I got near enough to see that it came through a small *grille*, or iron door, which terminated the branch of the sewer in which I was. When I reached the grating, I saw that it looked out upon the river, between which and it, however, there lay a deep indentation, or channel, of some fifty or sixty yards in length. It was gray morning, and I could see boats and steamers and ships, passing and repassing upon the river. Surely deliverance was now at hand! but how was I to make my situation known? My voice, as I have said, was utterly gone, and I had barely strength left to wave my pocket-handkerchief from the grating. There I stood for hours, — a prisoner looking wistfully through the bars of a dungeon to which no wayfarer came. I had sunk down at the foot of the grating, from mere exhaustion, when the whining of my little dog attracted me, and I gave him a caressing pat. He licked my face and whined again, as much as to say, "Can't I be of some use to you?" This brought a bright idea to my mind. Tearing a leaf from my note-book, I wrote the following words upon it, with pencil: —

"I have lost my way in the sewers. You will find me at the grating just opposite a large buoy marked X. Come quickly."

Placing this inside my india-rubber tobacco-pouch, I bound it tightly, with a strip from my pocket-handkerchief, to Dane's collar; and then, taking the little fellow gently in my arms, and speaking a word or two of dog-talk to him, I dropped him from the grating into the stream below, which was running out fast enough to prevent him from trying to return; nor was it long before I had the satisfaction of seeing him swimming boldly out toward the river, as if he knew perfectly well what he was about. I had no fears but that somebody in a boat would pick him up before he was exhausted, because this kind of dog can live for a great while in the water. Yet he was gone for a long, long time, — at least, it seemed a long time to me, — and I saw the distant boats passing and repassing, and the steamers and the ships, and heard the cheery voices of the mariners, as I held on there by the iron grating, half-dead. At last a boat, pulled by two men and steered by a third, shot up into the channel; and the boatmen raised a joyful shout as I waved my handkerchief to them from my prison-bars. The steersman held my little dog upon his knee; but the faithful animal broke away from him when he saw me, and would have jumped overboard in his eagerness to reach me had he not been caught by one of the men.

When the boat had come quite close under the grating, I saw that it was manned by men of the river guard. They told me that one of their number had gone round to report the matter to the proper authorities, and that assistance would quickly be at hand, and one of them, standing on the thwarts of the boat, reached up to me a flask of brandy and a biscuit, after having partaken of which I felt sufficiently revived to be very thankful for my escape from a horrible death. In less than an hour keys were brought by an officer connected with the sewers, and I was released from my disagreeable position, much to the joy of Dane, who covered me with caresses after his honest doggy fashion; nor, half-starved as the little animal must have been, would he touch a morsel of biscuit until after he had seen me safe in the boat.

The next thing to be done was to make a search for Simonet, who had not made his appearance in the upper regions since we entered the sewers. Men were sent after him, and he was found in a half-stupefied condition just where I had left him, among the dead rats. He could give little or no account of himself, save that his torch had gone out, just as he was about starting in search of me, and that a stupor came over him, then, and he sat down and fell asleep. This was all accounted for afterwards. Having lost his pipe, as I have said, he sought to assuage his craving for stimulants by chewing — or rather eating — quantities of the tobacco with which I had furnished him, and this proved, on examination, to have been taken by me, in mistake, from a jar in which opium had been copiously mixed with the milder narcotic for experimental purposes. Probably the little I had smoked of it in my pipe had somewhat affected me; and Simonet averred that he thought it must have been the smell of it that saved us from being eaten by the rats. A few franc pieces, a new pipe, and a reasonable stock of the best tobacco, made a happy man of that rare old gutter-snipe; but nothing could induce him to make any further reference to the white rat, at the very mention of which he would scowl horribly, and retire, as it were, behind the mass of red hair with which his face was fringed.

As for me, I believe more in horse-shoes than ever, since the adventure narrated above. I had a small one made in silver, for Dane; and this the faithful animal wore suspended from his collar as a charm until he went the way of all dogs, full of honors and of years.

www.ingramcontent.com/pod-product-compliance
Lightning Source LLC
LaVergne TN
LVHW022039110826
845151LV00007B/929

9781425530532